THE LEGACY SERIES

The Correct Response
Manfred Gabriel

Welcome Back to the World: A Novella & Stories
Rob Davidson

Greyhound Cowboy and Other Stories
Ken Post

Close Call
Kim Suhr

The Waterman
Gary Schanbacher

Signs of the Imminent Apocalypse and Other Stories
Heidi Bell

What We Might Become
Sara Reish Desmond

The Silver State Stories
Michael Darcher

An Instinct for Movement
Michael Mattes

The Machine We Trust
Tim Conrad

Gridlock
Brett Biebel

Salt Folk
Ryan Habermeyer

The Commission of Inquiry
Patrick Nevins

Maximum Speed
Kevin Clouther

Reach Her in This Light
Jane Curtis

The Spirit in My Shoes
John Michael Cummings

The Effects of Urban Renewal on Mid-Century America and Other Crime Stories
Jeff Esterholm

What Makes You Think You're Supposed to Feel Better
Jody Hobbs Hesler

Fugitive Daydreams
Leah McCormack

Hoist House: A Novella & Stories
Jenny Robertson

Finding the Bones: Stories & A Novella
Nikki Kallio

Self-Defense
Corey Mertes

Where Are Your People From?
James B. De Monte

Sometimes Creek
Steve Fox

The Plagues
Joe Baumann

The Clayfields
Elise Gregory

Kind of Blue
Christopher Chambers

Evangelina Everyday
Dawn Burns

Township
Jamie Lyn Smith

Responsible Adults
Patricia Ann McNair

Great Escapes from Detroit
Joseph O'Malley

Nothing to Lose
Kim Suhr

The Appointed Hour
Susanne Davis

"*The Mexican Messiah* is a strange and alluring search through doubt and desire toward unlikely grace. With shimmering, vibrant language, Kauffmann offers unexpected insights on the nature of fate and faith, conjuring a landscape where saguaros speak, visions of bare feet lead toward redemption, and 'nothing exists that is not divine.' A captivating journey of wonder."

—HARRISON CANDELARIA FLETCHER
Colorado Book Award Winner
author of *Finding Querencia: Essays from In Between*

"Jay Kauffmann has the grace to write about the nature of faith and belief, the emptiness of privilege, the baffled rage born of loss—all without passing judgment. In these rancorous and polarized times, his oddly beguiling fiction was surprising and welcome, and just what I needed."

—DIANE LEFER
author of *California Transit*
Mary McCarthy Prize Winner

"This polished, haunting collection is as cinematic as Sonoran Desert heat shimmer. Imagine a mysterious collaboration of Capote, Castaneda, and Jim Morrison. With echoes of Graham Greene and Paul Bowles, the mythos is nonetheless very much its own story—working across many kinds of borders."

—KRIS SAKNUSSEMM
author of *Zanesville*

"In his debut collection, Jay Kauffmann takes his readers on a whirlwind trip around the world, getting lost with a smattering of souls only looking to be found. It's a funny, tense, and exhilarating collection, culminating in the title novella, a thrilling and surprising last leg. *The Mexican Messiah* is an unforgettable launch for an exciting new voice."

—MICHAEL CZYZNIEJEWSKI
author of *The Amnesiac in the Maze*

"Riveting and cinematic, here are tales with echoes and elements of Denis Johnson and Cormac McCarthy."

—TIM WENDEL
author of *Rebel Falls*

"Jay Kauffmann's *The Mexican Messiah* is a suspenseful and vividly realized tale—one for our contemporary moment—of religious mystery and seeking, of the desperate desire for connection and healing, set against the fear of charlatanism, loneliness, and failed hope. Kauffmann's lean prose and arrestingly compressed scenes bring his portraits of characters on the edge to life with striking force."

—ELISE LEVINE
author of *Say This: Two Novellas*

"Perhaps the most geographically diverse collection I've ever read—from the North Pole to the Sahara Desert and many places between—the stories in Jay Kauffmann's *The Mexican Messiah* explore lives that have become shallow and meaningless—characters confronting the loss of love, family, community, and fulfillment. All of them seek a solution to their overwhelming sense of emptiness, dealing with a culture whose values are limited to power, sex, and wealth, full of memorable characters, electric dialogue and vivid descriptions. Fun and engaging all the way through. A must read."

—JIM PETERSON
author of *The Sadness of Whirlwinds*

"Reminiscent of Cormac McCarthy, this haunting collection will move you as much by what is left out as what is included as the trajectories of its central characters collide. Jay Kauffmann has given us a rich narrative that attempts to answer unanswerable questions about love and, especially, loss."

—CLIFFORD GARSTANG
author of *The Last Bird of Paradise*

THE MEXICAN MESSIAH

A NOVELLA & STORIES

JAY KAUFFMANN

CORNERSTONE PRESS
UNIVERSITY OF WISCONSIN-STEVENS POINT

Cornerstone Press, Stevens Point, Wisconsin 54481
Copyright © 2025 Jay Kauffmann
www.uwsp.edu/cornerstone

Printed in the United States of America by
Point Print and Design Studio, Stevens Point, Wisconsin

Library of Congress Control Number: 2025934059
ISBN: 978-1-960329-82-0

Cornerstone Press titles are produced in courses and internships offered by the Department of English at the University of Wisconsin–Stevens Point.

DIRECTOR & PUBLISHER
Dr. Ross K. Tangedal

EXECUTIVE EDITORS
Jeff Snowbarger, Freesia McKee

EDITORIAL DIRECTOR
Brett Hill

SENIOR EDITOR
Ellie Atkinson

PRESS STAFF
Logan Benkstein, Paige Biever, Eliot Javers, Ankica Montgomery, Anthony Thiel, Sam Zajkowski, Sophie McPherson, Madison Schultz, Autumn Vine, Ava Willett

For Taliesin,
Emerson,
and Jules

CONTENTS

Where you come from is gone.

—Flannery O'Connor

I am in the hands of the unknown god,
he is breaking me down to his own oblivion.

—D. H. Lawrence

To find the soul it is necessary to lose it.

—A. R. Luria

The Prince of Denmark

I.

Two weeks with a madman and nothing but cigarettes and fish soup, cold, choppy waters, and bile rising and falling within you as the ship rides the waves. Within a hundred nautical miles of the North Pole, you wonder how you agreed to this.

"Forget me, forget everything," says Sebastian, the photographer, launching into his morning pep talk. "You are not a model. You are a fisherman—who loves to smoke. Don't pose, don't act, just be, live as the fisherman." He hands you a fishing pole. "Now smoke."

The wind is fierce, your hands numb. You fumble with the lighter, drop your cigarette. The assistant passes you a lit one, unfiltered. "Watch the clothes," says the stylist. You have already burned two holes in your cable-knit sweater. Above, the mainsail flaps and lulls, the wind undecided. Blood red with giant white letters, the sail reads: *Prince of Denmark Cigarettes.* Everything is blood red: your clothes, your shoes, the trim of the ship. They even brought along an Irish setter, which lies limp on deck, lifting its head only to retch.

It's high summer—3 AM—though it feels more like the dead of winter. Infernal days—the sun never fully goes down. It only bobs briefly on the horizon before beginning to rise again.

"Ach, das Licht!" says Sebastian. *"Unglaublich schön!"*

He points the camera at you, fires off a few rolls. You bite down on the cigarette and flash a smile.

"Nein! Nein!" He shakes his head, pursing his lips in that oddly German manner, and exhales. "You still don't understand, do you? None of that model crap. Simple. No tricks. Just be. Okay? Can you do that for me?"

You nod. Banners of crimson light arc over your head. You start again, staring heroically out over the water, taking a long drag, still astonished by the tobacco's foul, bitter taste. Smoke funnels out of your nostrils. You begin to cough, lightly at first, then uncontrollably, while the nausea gathers force. Soon you are hanging over the edge of the ship, moaning, eyes watering, torrents of fish soup, coffee, Saltines, half-digested seasick pills gushing out of you.

The photo team turns away, giving you a moment to regroup. The thought of smoking another cigarette sets off the gagging reflex again. You lied through your teeth at the casting—"Smoked for years," you said—when, in point of fact, you had had maybe two cigarettes in your life. At an average of eight packs a day, you wonder if cancer can strike in two weeks.

You were thrilled when you first heard about the job. The photographer was famous, cutting-edge, known for sepia-toned images of gaunt, bug-eyed girls strutting across the desert. And the money was good—your day rate plus ten grand for every picture used. But then you began to think: cigarettes killed your father at fifty-three, scorched his throat and lungs as if by wildfire. How could you allow yourself to promote the very thing that fucked up your life?

But here you are, nevertheless, wondering if you still have an ethical bone in your body, buffeted between waves of greed and guilt.

Off starboard a small killer whale, about the size of an SUV, rolls over on its back, showing its white belly. *"Schaut mal!"* cries Sebastian, pointing, frenetic. "Get him out there!" He turns to you, his eyes bloodshot and pinwheeling. It occurs to you he is either drugged or demented—perhaps both. "You—James. Get into the dinghy."

"Huh?" You want to sit down and discuss this a moment, consider all the variables, when at once you are hustled over to a small rowboat hanging off the side of the ship.

"Keep rowing," offers the assistant, handing you a cigarette. "You'll stay upright."

"What about a life vest?" you ask, as they slowly lower you—turning a pair of cranks—into the swells. No one answers. A second whale has been spotted, the two rolling together, cavorting, displacing mountains of water. The hull smacks against the surface. The last of the rope pulls through its rings. Suddenly you are adrift.

"Okay," shouts Sebastian, "get as close to them as you can."

You begin flailing the oars, puffing madly on your cigarette, drenched in sea-spray. The dinghy bobs like a child's toy. The whales draw closer, circling, then darting beneath you, as the dinghy shudders and spins and freefalls before popping up again. One of the whales glides leisurely along next to you. For a few seconds, its massive eye, glistening like crude oil, fixes on you, and you see yourself, your reflection, as the whale must see you—a helpless thing, lost, the color of fresh blood, possibly breakfast.

It gradually registers that Sebastian has been shouting at you—"More cool!"—and you realize your face is fixed in a mask of horror, the cigarette, now extinguished, dangling from your lower lip. You can see Sebastian bounding about on deck, his assistant continuously loading and feeding him cameras. *Cool,* you want to point out, *is no longer in your repertoire.*

One of the whales slaps its massive tail against the surface, dousing you in a sheet of water, then abruptly dives, followed by the other, and at once both whales are gone.

Sebastian hands the camera to his assistant and, almost as an afterthought, waves you back to ship. For an instant, you consider going on alone, making for the nearest shore, as you stare wistfully at the charcoal smudge on the horizon.

When you look back, the deck is clear except for Nathalie, the hair and make-up artist. *"Quelle catastrophe!"* she shrieks. *"Regarde-toi! Viens là . . . allez, vite.* We must re-make you, *tout de suite."*

You drop anchor off the coast of a small, hilly island about the size of two city blocks, bare but for patches of gray rock and fluorescent grass. The photo team begins climbing down into the rowboats. Suddenly, on a whim, delirious to be going ashore, you leap from the deck and land hard on the dinghy below.

"You crazy or what?" cries the assistant. *"Scheiße,* you almost landed on me!"

Sebastian smiles. "Do it again," he says.

"Nein, Sebastian . . ." protests the assistant.

Sebastian shoots him a look. *"Genug,"* he says as if scolding a child, then orders everyone back on deck.

Soon you are standing once more on the edge of the ship, looking down upon the bobbing dinghy, the faces of Sebastian and his assistant staring up at you—camera poised.

Idiot! And you jumped why, exactly? You light up, taking a moment to observe the cigarette, which—drawing life from your breath—appears to delight in its own destruction.

"I want to see you fly!" says Sebastian who, you realize, has let himself drift, so that an alarming expanse of water now lies between you and the dinghy.

You shake your head. "No way, man. Get closer or forget the whole thing."

You can see his jaw clench then grind as if chewing on something. "But, James," he says, "this is it! I can feel it. This is the shot. You—flying through the air like a fucking phoenix. All over Europe. Magazines, buses, billboards. Think about it. I'm going to turn you into a god." He closes his eyes, as if picturing it, nodding in appreciation.

It's ninety percent crap, but that ten percent has got you thinking. It would be something. But worth breaking a leg, going into hypothermia? Behind, you can feel the eyes of the team on you.

"Listen, James, forget it. If you don't want to do it, don't do it. *Kein Problem* ... I'll just fly in another model tomorrow."

Bastard! The leap is one thing, landing quite another. Gripping the cigarette squarely between your teeth, you take three steps back and assume a sprinter's pose. "You ready?" you call out. "I'm only doing this once, so you better be"—adding under your breath, "you crazy son of a bitch."

"*Ja, ja.* Ready."

"*Attends,*" cries Nathalie, running up behind you. She adds some mousse to your hair and tosses it like a salad. "*Bon voyage, chéri.*"

As you arc out over the water, you become intensely aware of details—the hard glare, the goosebumps on the back of your neck, the taste of cigarettes and salt, the gusts of cold air rising. Arms spread wide, legs like a pendulum, you bear down on the small dinghy. With little hand movements and hip adjustments, you try to direct your fall into the black maw of the photo lens. You have, however, overshot the boat slightly. The realization comes, surprisingly, with a sense of resignation. There is really nothing you can do. Sebastian and his assistant duck, shielding themselves with their arms, as you sail by overhead. Your right foot clips the gunwale—the pain searing—which flips you end over end into the sea.

"*Schweinegeil!*" says Sebastian as they row up alongside you. "I've made you into a *gottverdammte* deity today. You hear me, James? Like Jesus or Krishna—only cooler. You'll double your rate. People will stop you on the street. You should be grateful. Hell, you should kiss my fucking feet."

The cold is so devastating you cannot speak, can barely breathe. Though numbed, you are certain your foot, or maybe your ankle, is broken. But why is no one pulling you out of the water? For an instant, you seem to have blacked out, because your reality comes shockingly back into focus.

The assistant grabs your arm.

"Einen Moment," says Sebastian.

"Was?"

Sebastian leans over the gunwale—to pull you out, you assume—his face inches away. "Don't look at me that way . . . with those disapproving fish eyes, you ungrateful *model* you"—the word contorts in his mouth like a slur. "You want magic, miracles? Well, I give it to you. Want to be rockstar hot? You got it. But don't expect it easy. Dramatic measures—that's what it takes. Nothing less. You should thank me. You understand? I have resurrected you from the ordinary. Now thank me."

"Sebastian, bitte," says the assistant. *"Es ist zu kalt."*

"Well?"

It gradually dawns on you that he is waiting for a response. Lips like jelly, you bark, "Whaaa?"

"Thank me."

You look to the assistant, his face like that of a whipped dog, then back to Sebastian. Another minute you may not survive. Gathering yourself, you kick down sharply and lunge, grabbing hold of Sebastian's collar. His jacket—blood red with *Prince of Denmark* across the front—is nothing but silk and feathers in your hand. As you sink back into the water, you twist and pull.

"Hilfe!" cries Sebastian, his face deliciously horrified, camera still slung around his neck. As he grips the gunwale, the boat begins to tip.

"Mein Gott, nein!" yelps the assistant.

"The film, James! Not the film!"

You almost have him, can feel the balance begin to shift, when, all at once, the collar tears, shearing away in your hand, as tiny white feathers, like snowflakes, swirl about you and float down delicately upon the water.

II.

September in Paris. Leaves scuttle over the cobblestones of the Marais like crabs. Parisians stride purposefully along the avenues, their tans faded, scarves flung around their necks with deliberate nonchalance. Chestnuts roasting on metal drums suffuse the air with a sweet, earthy smell. Your cast is off at last, though you still use a cane. The doctor recommended walking, so you go everywhere by foot. You cross the Seine, from right bank to left, weaving through the herds of tourists near Notre Dame, then begin the long climb up to the Sorbonne to meet Sophie.

Your mother called from Washington this morning. Strange you can't bring yourself to tell her about the campaign. But after everything she went through with your father. . . . As it is, she doesn't understand the modeling. She lies about you—you've heard her do it—tells her friends you're a businessman. Sophie, of course, supports you, whatever you do, though sometimes you wonder if that would still be the case if you could no longer afford the apartment on Place des Vosges, keep her in Kenzo and Dior.

You haven't worked since the Denmark job and worry that you might never work again, that you have gone out of style, grown too old, fat, thin—uncool. You know one day it will come. You can picture it: there you'll be, a bit paunchy and gray, hanging around at castings like a bad smell. You'll have to give up the fancy apartment, holidays in Greece, perhaps even Sophie. Then what?

You cross an intersection, the cane *click-click-clicking* against the pavement. The wind picks up and you zip shut the collar of your jacket.

Sebastian called the agency last week, said that you lied, that you had never smoked before, and it showed on film. He recommended that the client refuse to pay. The agency has set lawyers in motion.

You drag yourself along Rue des Écoles—vaguely intimidated by the high stone walls of the university—until you reach Place de la Sorbonne, where you find a quiet bench to wait for Sophie. Luminous, dark-haired and almond-eyed, with thick-rimmed glasses, she brings to mind a librarian from Persia. With only a semester left in her studies, she speaks now of nothing but travel. You are considering asking her to marry you but haven't yet found the courage.

You prop up your bad foot, which has begun to throb, and watch the students pass. A main point of rendezvous, the square swirls with young couples running up to one another and kissing. It's like watching the climactic scene of a dozen romantic films. They appear so vibrant and real, while you feel one-dimensional.

A light rain begins to fall as the smell of cordite rises from the street. Everyone scatters, then reconvenes, huddled beneath the awnings of the cafés. You remain on the square—the only one—as raindrops patter down on your shoulders. You recognize that some of the students are looking at you. You are briefly the subject of conversation—*the man who waits in the rain*. You can almost hear them, the disparate strains of dialogue: "Who's he waiting for? . . . What happened to him that he should need a cane? . . . He has *une bonne tête*—no? . . . Why won't he get out of the rain? . . . Perhaps a touch of madness about the eyes . . . Quite obviously American . . ."

You glance at your wristwatch to have something to do. She's late, by eleven minutes. You're starting to feel drenched now, hair flattened, rivulets running down your neck beneath your collar. You really should move, but you don't. You continue to sit there, suspended.

Just then one of those turquoise-colored Parisian buses pulls up alongside the square, brakes hissing, and there you are, pasted to its side: *The Prince of Denmark*. Arms reaching outward, legs together, you form a perfect, blood-red cross hanging in mid-air, like a Christ-figure—somehow both crucified and risen at the same time. The cigarette looks digitally enhanced, as do your eyes, which appear impossibly bright, the very shade of the sky. You look good, ridiculously good, heroic, maybe a little enraged, your jaw chiseled—airbrushed?—like leading men of the thirties. Sebastian was right, the bastard: it is an amazing shot, one in a million.

You turn to look for Sophie, to share your excitement, impress her, show her the optimum you. But the square is empty. When you look back, the bus has just left, and you watch yourself—that supreme version of yourself—drift away.

In the German Garden

The moment his plane touched down, Henry wondered if what he was doing made any sense. Would his son even want to see him again, let alone make an effort to reconcile? It was dawn in Berlin, a Saturday—or was it Sunday?—in August, the sky low and gray, with just a hint of light on the horizon. Henry ran a hand through his hair, which felt greasy after the long trip, and considered his lap where a tray of chicken Kiev had overturned. He slipped on his sport coat and buttoned it shut, though the stain was still visible.

The prospect of facing his ex-wife and her husband made him physically ill. Henry may have left Germany, but it was Martina who had left him. As he strolled down the bright, echoing hallway to passport control, he remembered, twenty years before, the first time he had arrived in Berlin. He was twenty-five, cocky, his uniform intentionally small to show off his physique. He had come with no illusions; then again, he didn't expect to be a flunky, either (administrative assistant, they called it) to that pompous tight-ass, Colonel Chamberlain. He could still smell the man's sweet pipe tobacco.

He entered Schoenefeld's vast hall, set down his bag, and waited—he hoped—for his son to appear out of the crowd. He wondered if a hug was appropriate after so many years. Michael was seven the last time Henry saw him, thin and pale, prone to bouts of giggling, with white-blond hair. Every morning they would bike to the bakery for *brötchen*, then race home, neck and neck till the finish, at which point Henry would touch his brakes and let him win.

He had always meant to be a better father. How many times had he invited the boy to Washington? Ten, twelve? But Martina always managed to come up with some excuse. There was summer school, *Fussball* camp, chicken pox. . . . In more recent years, it was simply: "He doesn't want to." Of course, Henry had meant to return, but somehow something had always come up. That was even how he explained it, lame as it sounded: "Sorry, pal, but something's come up." And though Henry wrote and called, it was sporadic. As he climbed the ranks—finally reaching (like Chamberlain, no less) full colonel—his military career took precedence. It's not that he stopped caring—there was always that longing, that throb of guilt—it's more that he was just so busy Michael invariably fell to the bottom of his list. And now he was seventeen—*Seventeen!*

Henry spotted a blond teenager moving in his general direction, wearing trainers and baggy sweats—*Michael?*—but, no, the youth stopped short of Henry and embraced an old woman—probably his grandmother. He hoped Michael would like his gift—the latest iPod, so new, in fact, the salesman had assured him, that no one in Europe would have one.

"Henry?"

Henry turned to face his ex-wife. Smiling, blond hair pulled taut against her skull, she hugged him with surprising warmth. She felt slimmer in his arms than he remembered. "Martina, I didn't expect . . ."

"Oh, you look so disappointed." She smiled. "Michael couldn't make it. But don't worry," she said, mimicking his glum expression, "you'll see him later."

She drove at an alarming speed, weaving through traffic with no apparent concern for lights or signs or other drivers, working the Mercedes's stick-shift like a cock, it seemed to him, which she wanted to dislodge.

"I've made a reservation at the Omni. I think it's on *Kurfürstendamm*."

"Nonsense," she said, eyes ahead. "You stay with us."

They drove along the *Grunewald*, sunlight streaming through the dense woods. They had met at a summer party near here, he remembered, in one of those old mansions once owned by Nazis. She couldn't believe he was in the army, she had said, he seemed too sensitive. She was in nursing school, crushingly voluptuous, full of Marxist ideas, spoke English like a Brit. How she loved turning everything he held true on its head. . . . There were stories about these woods, he recalled, about wild boars that mauled dogs, carried children away, even killed a jogger. She had teased him about it once while they were strolling through the dark forest, causing him to jump half out of his skin whenever a twig snapped.

"So, how is Michael?"

She rolled her eyes, exhaling. "Unbelievable. A whirlwind most of the time. Frankly, I can't keep up."

They stopped in front of a large, modern house made of steel and glass, surrounded by tall pines, designed by Franz, no doubt—her architect husband, the man she had left him for. Suddenly, there he was in the doorway, Franz, waving, pot-bellied and balding, still in his bathrobe—not in the least slick, nothing, really, like what Henry had imagined.

"Henry, *hallo*, please, please, come in." The man actually hugged Henry, took his bag out of his hand. "Hungry? *Ja, natürlich*. I prepared *frühstück*."

Henry felt guilty for all the times he had thought badly of the man.

After washing up and changing, Henry joined them around a large wooden table covered with dark bread and cheeses, *müesli* and yogurt, pots of tea and coffee.

"Well, well, here we are," said Franz.

"I hope this isn't too awkward—my being here and all."

Franz pursed his lips and frowned. "Why? Why should it be? Absolutely not . . ."

"Guten Appetit," said Martina, reaching across the table to stroke the back of Franz's hand.

They began to eat. Henry had forgotten how good a slice of bread could be. Outside, a half-dozen sparrows fluttered excitedly around the birdfeeder. It came to him then, out of nowhere, her reason for leaving him: "Please understand, Henry, I need to find my German self again." More at ease than he remembered, she seemed to have found it.

"How is Kirby?" she asked between sips of tea.

"Um, fine," said Henry, stunned that his present wife, her very existence, had momentarily slipped his mind. "She's taken up running."

"Oh, Americans are so sporty. I just can't with these . . ." She cupped her breasts in her hands.

Franz chuckled.

Henry looked at his wristwatch—embarrassed, threatened, turned on?—then, adding six, realized it was 11AM. "So, where exactly is Michael?"

"Sleeping," said Martina. "You didn't know? Welcome to the world of a teenager."

HENRY STOOD OVER Michael as he lay in bed, uncovered, face-down, wearing nothing but briefs. My son, he thought, stunned by the boy's size (close to six feet, he figured), his lean musculature. His hair was short, almost a military cut, light brown like Henry's. He sat down on the edge of the bed and placed his hand on Michael's tan shoulder. "Hey, pal," he whispered, "time to wake up. Your old man's here."

Michael groaned, stretched, rolled onto his back. His blue eyes stared without expression. Then, gradually, as they began to focus and recognize him, Henry watched his son's eyes imperceptibly harden.

Well, he knew it wasn't going to be easy.

Michael sat up and yawned. *"Morgen."*

Henry wanted to wrap his arms around the boy, smell him, *eat him up with a spoon*, as if he were still a toddler. But he held himself back, envisioning how his son would cringe. "Man, I missed you. You have no idea . . ."

"Ach . . . slow down." He shook his head in frustration. "My English is rusty."

"Right, sure, I'll let you wake up first." As Henry stood to leave, he passed his hand through Michael's hair, which felt bristly, like the end of a broom. Abstractedly, Michael reached up and brushed his hand away.

THEY SAT TOGETHER in silence, beneath the canopy of pines, forming a triangle—Michael, Henry and Martina. Now and then, a warm breeze passed over them, triggering a shower of needles. As Henry crossed and uncrossed his legs, the wicker chair squealed beneath him.

"Such a lovely day," said Martina. "Why don't you two go for a walk and catch up . . . or how about a bike ride? Yes, that's an idea. Henry, you can borrow Franz's bike."

"Where *is* Papa?" asked Michael.

Henry felt it like a blow.

"Michael," said Martina.

"It's alright," said Henry.

Michael leaned back and extended his legs, crossing them at the ankles. He wore a white T-shirt and jeans, freshly pressed. His bare feet looked enormous, a size twelve at least. He reminded Henry of an officer on leave, arrogant, carefree, a bit blasé.

"Oh, I almost forgot . . . I have something for you." Henry leaned forward, reached into the plastic bag at his feet, and withdrew a small white box with *Mac* emblazoned across the side. "Catch," he said, tossing the gift. Michael grabbed it out of the air and for an instant—as a look of wonderment passed over his face—Henry caught sight of the boy he once knew. He laughed, more for the release of it than anything else. "The salesman called it *cutting edge*."

Michael tore open the box, looked it over. "I already have one," he said, setting the iPod back in its box. "But thanks."

"But this is the newest version."

"Looks the same," said Michael.

"Well, it isn't."

Martina, to his right, reached over and patted his thigh. "How thoughtful, Henry."

Henry felt like a fool—infuriated, whether more with his son or the salesman he couldn't say. "Never mind," he said. "Give me the damn thing. I'll get you something else."

THE BOY HANDLED his chopsticks deftly, dipping his *maki* in *wasabi* then harvesting shaved ginger before tossing it into his mouth. His wristwatch looked expensive, absurdly so, far more than anything Henry could ever afford. He made a mental note to undo Martina's indulgences— starting immediately.

"How would you like to come live with me in Washington—just for a while, see how you like it? You could go to Georgetown. A hell of a school. I'm sure we could get you in . . ."

A slight smile, more a smirk, crept over Michael's face. "Mother will never agree."

"I don't see why not."

"Besides, I don't want to."

"Ah, well, that's a different story . . ."

They sat at a small table against the window. Dark and cramped, the restaurant reminded Henry of a compartment on a train. Outside, young nightclubbers strode past.

"Your mother says you're interested in politics. Is that right?"

"Hmm." He seemed bored, watching people go by.

"You're going to have to give me more than that."

He took a sip of tea. "Bush should be assassinated."

Henry laughed. "Why don't you say what you really think?"

Michael stared, soberly. "Forget bin Laden, your president—*your boss*—is the real terrorist."

"He's your president, too."

The boy's mouth fell open in a cartoon-like expression of horror, cheeks flaring red. "I refuse to be American."

Henry drew away, stunned by his son's rage, which he then understood to be directed at him. At the next table, two women held hands, smoking clove cigarettes. The smell left Henry feeling nauseous. He also felt jetlagged, as if swimming against a fierce current.

Rain began to pelt the sidewalk as hip, faintly punkish kids rushed past, boots slapping the pavement.

Michael considered his watch. "I have to go," he said, then stood and slipped on his leather jacket. "Tell mother I'll be home late."

"How late?"

"*Tschüss*," said Michael, ignoring him, and walked out.

A moment later, Henry left some money on the table and—surprised by his own impulsiveness—set off after his son.

ONCE ON THE STREET, he looked left and right, then spotted Michael, hunched against the rain, hands in his pockets, striding away. Henry followed from a distance. The boy wound his way through Kreuzberg, heading God knows where. The narrow cobblestone streets glistened like a river. Taxis rumbled past, the smell of diesel in the air. Henry felt ridiculous, vaguely criminal. After all, since when did stalking become acceptable parenting?

Michael stopped in front of a kebab shop and embraced— kissed on the mouth—a short mustachioed man in his twenties, Turkish looking. Henry ducked into a doorway.

It smelled of piss. He shivered, felt wet to the bone. The German word for fag—*Schwul*—popped into his head, though he remained surprisingly detached.

When he looked out again, he saw that they had crossed the street and joined a small crowd, bathed in bright bluish light, pressed in front of a nightclub beneath an awning which read: *The Blue Angel*. His son kissed and embraced more friends—girls as well as boys. Perhaps he wasn't gay, after all, thought Henry, reassured. Someone handed Michael a cigarette, no, a joint, from which he took a long drag then passed on. Every few seconds the club's door opened, releasing a deep throbbing beat that Henry felt in his abdomen.

A woman, clearly a prostitute, dressed in fishnet stockings and a leather bustier, walked past, then, noticing him, said, *"Hast du Lust zu ficken?"*

From the coarse timbre of the voice, Henry realized at once it was a guy, or rather a transsexual, for his breasts looked large and real-ish. "No . . . *Nein.*"

"Ah, you're American . . . I used to live in L.A."

Henry nodded, peering around the corner at Michael, who was still waiting to be let in, bobbing to the rhythm.

"Who are you watching?" The transsexual slipped in beside Henry, smelling of old woman's perfume, her shoulder-length hair plastered to her head and dripping.

Henry inched away.

"Oh, come on . . ." said the transsexual, craning her neck, "which one?"

Henry felt trapped, eager to flee yet unwilling to expose himself to Michael. "The tall boy in jeans and leather jacket."

"Mmm, *Schön!* And why are we spying on him?"

Henry faced the transsexual, whose nose was flat and twisted like a boxer's, and whose mascara ran down her cheeks in black rivulets. "For Christ's sake, go away."

"Ah, you're in deep—I can see it. And you wonder how you can make him love you again. Isn't that right?"

Henry realized at once it was true. When he looked back to where his son had been, he was no longer there.

CRYSTALLINE LIGHT SHONE through the woods, the sort of light that appears after a storm has swept the air clean. Henry followed Michael as they rode their bikes into the *Grunewald*, passing massive estates once owned by the Third Reich's elite, their gardens ravaged, some transformed into open pits.

"Boars," said Michael, nodding toward the damage.

They pedaled along one of the lakes, where dozens of people sunbathed naked in a field. One old couple, with pendulous body parts and great rolls of flesh, strolled hand-in-hand without the least self-consciousness.

They continued deeper into the woods, crossing an occasional jogger. The web of trails ran for miles in every direction. Within minutes, there was no one.

They slalomed through mud, bucked over roots, sluiced through puddles. Michael stood out of the saddle and hammered up a small rise. Henry strained to keep up, sweat dripping off his brow. "Hey, pal, ease up a little."

Michael stopped. Henry pulled alongside, panting. It was late afternoon, nearly dusk, the air warm and still. Shards of light filtered through the trees. The rich black earth smelled of decay.

"Jesus, you're going to give me a coronary."

Michael smirked. He did that a lot, Henry noted.

"Listen, Michael . . ." This was as good a time as any, he thought. "I want you to come live with Kirby and me. Give the States a try."

Michael snickered, passed a hand across his face—the German gesture for someone who's crazy. "*Du bist total verrückt.*"

"Your mother and I agree: things have gotten out of hand . . . Anyway, it's already been decided."

Michael stepped off his bike, letting it fall. "You can't make me."

"Michael, listen to me . . . I'm your father: I love you. But it's time you shaped up." He wiped the sweat from his eyes.

Michael balled his hands into fists. "*Du Arschloch*," he growled. "*Ich hasse dich*."

Before Henry could say another word, the boy straddled his bike and stomped on the pedals. As Michael bolted away, Henry watched him grow smaller and smaller till he disappeared.

FOR A LONG TIME he stood there, expecting his son to return at any moment. Then it began to turn dark. The forest seemed to expand and contract as if taking a breath. Wherever Henry turned, it looked the same. He set out with only a vague sense of which way he had come, the bike at his side, now and then stung in the face by a branch. Soon the blackness enveloped him.

He laughed out loud at the absurdity of his situation, then, hearing the faint echo, felt a chill come over him and shuddered. He reminded himself that he was in Berlin, not the Congo, which offered small consolation. Beneath the dense canopy of trees, he could make out his hand gripping the bike's chrome handlebar but little else. It was pointless to continue. He began to look for higher ground—one of the lessons he remembered from boot camp—a place to wait out the night.

He felt his way to a clearing atop a small hill, laid down the bike, and sat on the damp ground. For an instant, he pictured Michael, as in a snapshot, back home in Washington, smiling across the kitchen table.

The wind picked up. Treetops swayed, limbs creaking. A gamey smell drifted past.

Then he heard the boars—an unmistakable sound— rooting and snorting in the underbrush. It sounded like a half-dozen or more. A branch cracked and fell to the ground. He stood and searched for a rock or stick, then settled on the bike, wielding it back and forth several times. They drew nearer, squealing feverishly, as if having seized upon his scent. He had never been on a battlefield before—a career desk jockey—but imagined this was what it was like. His every fiber felt coiled and electric. He considered his options, trying to stay calm, lucid. He abandoned fleeing at once, envisioning how they would drag him down from behind. No, better to hold his ground. As they scrabbled up the hillside, he crouched behind the frame, holding it as a shield, and waited.

THEY SURGED OVER HIM like a current, knocking him down. Something metallic—a pedal?—dug into his thigh. One slobbered over his ear and neck, its soft, rubbery snout exploring, almost tenderly, before gouging his scalp with its tusk. They moved clumsily over and around him as big as cows. He lay on his side, curled up, keeping the bike on top of him. As they gnawed on the tires, he heard the high-pitched release of air. He lashed out with the frame, cursing them. They grunted angrily, stepping back, then reconvened, tearing at his clothes, dragging off a shoe.

Then, as abruptly as it began, it ended.

Henry pushed the bike aside and listened as their snorting, stump-legged shuffle faded in the distance. In increments, he let himself relax, then surveyed for injuries. Though bloodied and sore, he was essentially unharmed. He sat up, nearly vomited, then lay back again.

LONG BEFORE DAWN, Henry set out, limping with one shoe, pushing the bike on shredded tires, the woods veiled in blue fog. Eventually, he reached a road along a wide body of water and squatted at the water's edge. He washed his hands and face, looking up now and then to watch the sun bleed over the shoreline. A boat passed, its sail ablaze with blood-orange light.

Having made it through the long purgatorial night, Henry felt rejuvenated. He didn't want to go back. He could imagine the scenario: the police car sitting out front, Franz and Martina looking concerned and apologetic, and Michael looking sheepish and guilty and resentful for having to feel guilt. He rose and headed south along the byway, though he hardly cared about the direction. He was resigned now to whatever might come—from his son or otherwise.

A PACK OF CYCLISTS streaked past, followed by a line of cars. Then a beat-up Trabant pulled alongside, its windows down, George Michael blaring.

"Hi there, stranger," said the driver. "Need a lift?" It took Henry a moment before he recognized the transsexual. "Honey, we won't bite." The car was full: *four transsexuals in a Trabant*—which sounded like the start of joke. She looked him up and down. "Looks like you've had quite a night."

They stuffed the bike in back, the trunk propped open, then made room for him in the backseat. He wedged between the two transsexuals, their breasts pressing up against him, the car smelling like a cross between a perfumery and a locker room. The one to his left was three inches taller than Henry and built like a wrestler, while the one to his right looked almost pretty, vaguely like Nathalie Wood.

"Where to?" said the driver.

"Well, I don't know . . ." said Henry. "I am a bit hungry."

"I know just the place—best bakery in Berlin . . . Of course, I really shouldn't. A girl's got to watch her figure, you know. But for you, just this once . . ."

"*Quatsch*, don't listen to her," said Nathalie Wood. "She'd fuck you for a *strudel.*"

They followed the water till they reached an intersection and cut through a wealthy residential area. As the car rumbled over cobblestone streets, they passed a joint around between them, a mixture of tobacco and hash. Henry took a hit, something he hadn't done in twenty years. What the hell, he thought, smiling to himself, I deserve a little R&R. Then, by chance, they passed in front of the house.

There, standing in the garden with the policeman, were Franz, Martina and Michael. As the car shot past, Michael looked up. Thrilled despite everything to see his son, Henry reached across the mounds of silicone to wave. Though he couldn't say in that brief moment if Michael recognized him or not, he did, however tentatively, raise a hand.

Sumo

The sumo wrestlers faced off like bulls, grunting, scuffing their feet, slapping their great thighs, hams of flesh trembling. Clouds of sand rose about them, the air rank with sweat and cigarette smoke. M. and I sat in the front row, on one side a Yakuza boss (finger missing), on the other a famous politician—the seats a gift from one of M.'s rich and powerful admirers. It was a significant bout: the new champion versus the old, each representing a different style, a different era.

The old champion was one of the biggest wrestlers the sport had ever seen. He had been groomed in the old way, eating enormous quantities of whale fat, his trainers rousing him from sleep to fit in extra meals. He had been trained to slam his fists, later his entire body, into concrete over and over again until he felt nothing, until he was nothing but callus. Lumbering grotesquely, jowls quavering, he needed three handlers to help him up into the ring. The new champion appeared small and lean in comparison, each muscle visible beneath a thin layer of fat, his face chiseled, handsome in the way of leading men. His preparation was revolutionary: he ran, lifted weights, ate beef. In gossip magazines he appeared with a beautiful woman on each arm. Then there was the added dimension: the old champion had been born in Hawaii. This more than anything—the fact that he was a foreigner—stirred emotions.

The referee raised his arm. The audience drew silent, leaning forward in their seats, the hall contracting to the brilliant ring of sand. The wrestlers adjusted their loincloths, sank lower into their squats. Each raised a leg and stomped it to the ground, raising more sand, then slapped their thighs and shouted—a nod toward tradition—to awaken the warrior within.

It was hard not to like the new champ. He was just so damn good-looking, an aura of glamour and effortlessness clinging to him. Though my heart went out to the old champ. A few years beyond his prime, he was a monument to another time, to a life of sacrifice.

When the referee dropped his arm, the wrestlers raced toward each other like freight trains.

The audience exploded. Despite his size, the old champ moved with astonishing speed. Barely able to walk, he now flew—a wall of flesh catapulted across the ring. Lithe, cat-like, the new champ sprang forward, ducking his shoulders low like an American football player. Upon impact, there was a terrific noise, like thunder, and for a moment it was as if all the air were sucked from the room. The new champ struck the old low and to the side, spinning him counter-clockwise. Wheeling his arms, the old champ righted himself and slapped his great paw against his opponent's neck. The new champ dropped to one knee, shaking his head as if to clear it. As the old champ moved in, the new one struggled to his feet, and they clasped each other like lovers—a freakish sculpture by Rodin—faces inches apart, motionless but for their arms which bulged and shifted in slow increments.

M. turned to me. "Oh, God, he's going to lose!" Like most of the women in the hall, she wanted the handsome one to win.

So I cheered for the Hawaiian.

"Bastard!"

The Yakuza boss and politician also wanted the handsome one to win, groaning and covering their eyes as the old champ drove the new one toward the edge of the ring.

How easily the audience turned, preferring this new pop star warrior, when the old champ had worked so hard to embrace the past, to be accepted. Never mind that he had lived in Japan since he was two, he would always be the *gaijing*. Some part of me—it was complicated—identified with the old champ. I knew alienation, knew what it was like to be an outsider—in a foreign land, a foreign career, a foreign self. That was me up there (as I flinched and sweated in my seat), the leviathan, straining within great folds of flesh, wanting nothing more than to crush the pretty boy.

I turned to M., hollered: "A thousand yen says the monster wins." It was like play money, anyway.

"You're on!"

We shook.

"Mister Studly's going down."

She frowned, pulled her hair back behind her ears—revealing diamond studs (a gift from another admirer)—and rolled up her sleeves as if she were about to leap up and join them.

The old champ pounded his giant mitts, open-palmed, against the new champ's chest, driving him still farther backward. Of course he would win—if only to validate *me*, and outcasts everywhere.

But then: a burst of motion. The new champ sank and spun with the deftness of a dancer, harnessing his opponent's mass and propulsion, then, with a flick of his wrist, hurled him from the ring.

He landed before us: a sprawling mass, bloodless, in a pool of sweat, reeking of ammonia. The audience rose to its feet, celebrating, while I remained in my seat, crestfallen, studying the old champ. He didn't move for a moment, then stared up from the concrete floor, eyes out of focus, face slack and lumped to one side like a slab of clay. He looked like he had just woken from a terrible dream. I felt sorry for him as he struggled to lift himself up onto his hands and knees. Where were his handlers, for God's sake? Then, for a moment, he stared at me, though I'm sure I was just a blur. Can I say this without sounding like a fool? I saw it in his eyes: *truth*. Those eyes—glazed, forlorn, nearly shut—seemed to speak to me: *This is not your life*, they seemed to say. *You've lost your way. Forsaken your gifts, your humanity. The money, hype—all of it has only turned you into an asshole. And in case you were wondering, your girlfriend is cheating on you.*

It had been two years since I left the States, since I fell into modeling as into a vat of oil. I was lucky. People began to recognize me, women to proposition me. I became flush beyond my dreams. And yet it all seemed illusory—like watching a film. Even M. was an illusion—cool, unreachable. Sometimes I thought about going home, only to realize that it, too, had become an illusion.

Just then, his handlers swarmed in, draped a robe over his shoulders, and helped him to his feet. Then, wiping a string of drool from his mouth, they steered him like a zeppelin from the hall. As he left, the audience applauded, though it seemed like pity.

When I turned toward M., she was on her feet, talking with the politician, slipping into her nightclub-hostess persona. He handed her his business card, flashed a predatory smile. Those curves, the yellow hair—she drove them mad without meaning to.

The audience erupted in a new round of applause as the current champ now left the hall, a wake of schoolgirls following closely behind.

M. turned to me abruptly, tossing the politician's card to the ground. "Let's get out of here." She grabbed me by the hand, and we joined the crowd pushing toward the exit.

"What happened?"

"Nothing." Though she said it with an edge.

When we finally got out of the hall, the night was cool and clear. A long line of taxis waited out front, the drivers in pristine white gloves.

"He said he wanted to lick my pussy."

"Jesus, you're kidding . . ." I looked at her, trying to appear more outraged than I was. It happened to her more often than it should.

The wind picked up as trash skidded and spiraled over the sidewalk.

"Ever think about leaving?" I said.

"Why . . .where?"

"How about Hawaii, or Bali, the Maldives maybe."

The famous politician and his entourage came out of the building. M. saw him then looked away—as if *she* had something to be ashamed of. All at once, now, without warning, I did feel outrage. It came over me with startling ferocity. Before I could even think about what I was doing, I started toward the politician—as if crossing into a ring— and called out: "Hey, asshole . . .yes, you, what did you say to my girlfriend?"

M. grabbed me by the arm. "Shhh . . .what are you doing!"

The politician and his crew, everyone in fact on the side- walk, turned to look at me. The politician waved, recognizing M.: "Herro, brondie . . ." He looked a bit drunk as he stag- gered into a bodyguard.

I continued barreling toward him, relishing the fury inside, the utter indifference to consequences. At last, there was no barrier between me and the world: *this was real.* "So let me hear you say it, you fuck."

It seemed to dawn on the politician now what was going on, because he grew very still and squatted, taking a warrior stance, belly drooping over his waistband. He slapped his thighs a few times. Then, loosening his tie, he reared back his head and bellowed like a bull.

Without fully realizing it, I stopped and squatted, too. We were about twenty feet apart, staring at each other. Somewhere behind me, M. was calling my name. I had forgotten what I was fighting for. It no longer mattered. I only knew I had to crush him. Suddenly, I felt enormous, bolstered, as if padded within layers of flesh. As the bodyguards closed in, I charged.

Sane

The border beyond which everything loses meaning . . .
is not miles away, but a fraction of an inch.

—Milan Kundera

I.

As the story went, Giovanni took one look at Maria and thought, *Sweet Jesus, this is the one!* She was so charged with passionate energy her body seemed hardly able to contain it. It appeared to express itself through her hair, rising up out of her head, Medusa-like, and cascading over her shoulders in luxuriant black curls. They were only teenagers when they first met and fell in love, still in school together in the small hill village west of Palermo.

They married soon after high school and Giovanni began work in his father's cobbler shop. With their parents' help, they bought a small house, a few chickens and goats. In the coming years, his father retired, leaving Giovanni the business, and he quickly earned a reputation as one of the best shoemakers in the region, far superior to his father. He studied the fashion magazines from Milano and copied the latest styles from the big designers up north. People began to make special trips from Palermo to buy his shoes. They came daily in their fancy cars, barreling down the single dirt lane, trailing a cloud of dust through the hills a mile long. He soon found that he could charge his clients from Palermo almost anything—ten, fifty, one hundred times what the shoes were worth. Gradually, he found himself becoming rich by village standards, respected. Then, after years of trying, Maria finally became pregnant. As his son Antonio slid from Maria's womb out into the world, wailing with all the life force of some infant deity, Giovanni shook his head in wonder, unable to believe his good fortune. What in God's name had he done to deserve such grace?

Had he known about Maria's family history, it's doubtful Giovanni would have done anything different. His love for her was primal, instinctual, transcendent. She only had to throw a glance—her sleepy, almost oriental eyes imploring from beneath droopy lids—and he would have done anything, rearranged chromosomes, to please her. Even to Giovanni she had always remained a mystery. She seldom spoke but to tell him what her heart had to say, as if it were something separate inside her with its own thoughts and whims. Sometimes it alarmed him how deeply she felt things—the dead sparrow that crashed into the kitchen window, the Sicilian farmers that went bankrupt from drought—and yet she never appeared particularly fragile. She reminded him of an olive tree: ancient, grounded, sensitive to the slightest current of air.

Perhaps if he had recognized the signs he could have done something to help. He should have known that something was wrong when she began setting up altars in every room of the house, nailing Francis of Assisi to the door. She had never been particularly devout, but suddenly she was spending hours at church, mumbling prayers long into the night. Then one afternoon Giovanni came home from work to find everything they owned had been dragged out onto the street and Maria offering it to the villagers, parceling it off like the body of Christ.

The next day it was her own body she was giving away. Giovanni found her wandering the streets, naked, giggling like a child, cupping her exquisite breasts in her hands and proffering them to each man she passed. A few days later she shut Antonio, who was five at the time, into the trunk of the car, because, she explained, his whining distracted her from her prayers. There was no telling how long his son had been lying there in the sweltering heat, pounding and screaming, before Giovanni finally let him out. After that, Giovanni closed his shop to stay home and watch her.

Then, early one morning, Giovanni woke, opened his eyes, and saw Antonio standing beside his bed.

"Where's Mama?" he asked.

Giovanni sat up, alert at once. "I don't know," he said. "Why don't we find her."

They searched the house, then the garden, and finally the surrounding hills. At last they found her squatting beneath an olive tree, covered in dirt and blood, her nightgown shredded and billowing in the wind. She was digging savagely at the earth with her bare hands, alternately spitting and cursing and keening like an animal. A kitchen knife lay in the dirt at her feet. He could see where she had tried numerous times to plunge the knife through her breast plate to reach her heart—that heart that had always spoken to her and now must have begun telling her unimaginable things.

II.

As he did most nights, Antonio sat at the edge of Jack's bed and watched him sleep, stroking his forehead, smoothing the blond curls. He still couldn't get over it: a Sicilian with blond hair! It was startling how much he loved his son. He never dreamed he could love anyone so much. Sonya often said he spoiled Jack, said he needed to be firmer with the boy, and though he knew she was right, he could never bring himself to scold him with any conviction. He found himself getting teary-eyed and pinched the bridge of his nose to curb the tears. He looked around the room at the toys strewn across the floor, at the pale blue nightlight, which always made him feel like he was at the bottom of the ocean.

Seeing Jack this way—so innocent and vulnerable—never failed to trigger in Antonio his fears for all that might await his son. He himself had turned out fine, thank God—depressed now and then but only in relation to life's compulsory disappointments. Still, there was no guarantee for his son. Maria's madness might be simmering within him this very moment, having only skipped a generation as a cruel joke.

He remembered, long before Jack was born, telling Sonya about his mother and her family, though the details of Maria's father and ancestors remained so buried in deception and shame Antonio would never know the full truth. He had wanted Sonya to know the risks before they had a child. Somewhere in the back of his mind he knew even his decision to marry Sonya was at least partially due to her Swedish heritage. He wanted to make sure his wife's bloodline was radiantly sane and as far from Sicily and his own bloodline as possible.

"Please, no more stories," Sonya had said. "I get the point. I still want to have your baby."

He had hugged her then, he recalled, and reassured her: "Any child born from such love can only be perfect."

He rarely thought of his mother anymore, shut away in an asylum, had tried not to think of her in the more than forty years since he and his father had emigrated to New York. He was American now, his past far behind him. And yet, over the last four years, since Jack was born, he found himself remembering her with greater frequency, watching for signs in Jack, similar traits, something that might point to the illness.

Gradually, he began to summon details of his mother's face—the beauty mark on her right cheek, the delicate worry lines and crow's feet, the fierce compassion in her eyes. He felt at once both anger and longing, aching with all that remained unresolved. As he sat there remembering her—shivering slightly as if a cold wind had passed over him—Antonio continued to stroke Jack's forehead, repeating under his breath, "Hail Mary, full of grace . . ."

"MUSIC, DADDY."

"What's the magic word?"

"Please."

"You got it, Bubba."

Antonio switched on the car radio and continued along Woodhaven—nothing but ads and news—then shut it off.

"Music," Jack cried. "*Music!*"

"Whoa. Easy, pal."

Antonio looked into the rearview mirror and could see tears starting to form in his son's eyes. He began to fumble with the dial and finally found a classical station. But he knew whatever he did now would be too little too late, as Jack worked himself up into a tantrum. He pulled into the parking lot in front of the kindergarten and waited. There was no point reasoning with him or demanding that he stop. He had tried all that before. The only thing to do was ignore him, wait for it to pass.

He left the car running with the heat on and stared out at the parking lot. It was autumn. Leaves scuttled over the pavement. A cold light played over the hood and dash. His son continued to rage, kicking the back of Antonio's seat, screaming himself hoarse.

Could this be normal?

Suddenly, with remarkable clarity, Antonio remembered the day his mother had locked him inside the trunk of the car—the darkness and isolation, the unbearable heat, the sense of having done something terribly wrong.

He slumped over the steering wheel and quietly wept.

"Daddy?" Jack said in a small voice.

Antonio found himself gasping for air, the silence around him closing in, humming like insects. At once, he flung open the door.

He stood there in the parking lot as the wind buffeted against him, wiping his eyes, trying to compose himself.

At last he spoke: "Let's go, Jack. You'll be late for school."

ANTONIO PULLED into the worksite. It had rained the night before and mud was everywhere. They'd have to whitewash the walls before they were done. He noticed how the moment his car turned into the lot everyone went into motion; instantly, their expressions turned earnest, committed. Paolo, the foreman, waved to Antonio and started over. He was Italian, already in the country fifteen years, and would never lose his accent.

"Tony, he is back again."

"Who?"

"Your special friend." He laughed. "Mister Bagman."

"Oh, Christ."

"Want me to handle it?"

"No, I'll talk to him."

He walked into the building, what would eventually become a health spa—in Queens of all places. The man was squatting in a corner of the building wrapped in sheets of clear plastic which he had pulled from the window frames. A half-dozen giant green trash bags stuffed with God knows what surrounded him. He was a surprisingly big man, not in the least gaunt or thin-limbed, bearded, eyes like a bloodhound's. And he had what looked like a homemade tattoo on his forehead, the letters jagged and uneven, which read: *Jesus*. He had appeared a few days before and Antonio had threatened to call the cops, thought he had scared him off for good, but he seemed more at home than ever.

"Okay, bud, out you go."

The man looked up, using his forlorn eyes to their full effect.

"No excuses. Just move it."

He busied himself stuffing the plastic sheets into his bags. The odor coming off him was like something decomposing.

"*Now!*" said Antonio.

The man struggled to his feet as an empty bottle of Jim Beam skated across the floor. Dragging his numerous bags, he shuffled toward the doorway. Antonio followed closely behind. Abruptly, the man stopped and turned. Even stooped, he looked down upon Antonio.

"Be careful," the man said, his diction remarkably clear and precise. "I know what's inside. Just a thin line between us."

"What?"

"Bad . . . bad . . . bad, I tell you. Nothing to keep you from hell but a handbasket full of shit and feathers."

"Okay, I've been nice so far . . ."

"One moment"—he snapped his fingers—"and it all changes."

It was getting dark when Antonio pulled up in front of his house and waved to his next-door neighbor raking leaves. "Daddy's home," called Sonya as he walked into the kitchen. He could hear Jack's footsteps closing in.

"Hey, hey, Jack Rabbit, what's shakin'?"

Jack leapt into his arms, the collie barking at his feet.

"Quiet, girl, that's enough," said Sonya as she embraced Antonio, Jack between them.

"I'm a sandwich," Jack said.

"Hmm, good," said Antonio, nibbling his ear. "Jack sandwich."

Jack dissolved in a fit of giggles.

"So how was your day?" she asked.

"Over, thank God." He smiled.

The world hadn't spun off its axis, after all, he thought—everything still as it should be.

A FEW DAYS LATER, the bagman was back. Some of the workers were taunting him as Antonio walked into the building.

"Hey, Jesus, so what's in the bag?"

"Yeah, what you got in there—besides more bags?"

Huddled, cowering, the man shielded himself with his arms.

"Let's just take a look-see." A new carpenter, someone Antonio hadn't bothered to get to know yet, reached for one of the bags.

The man recoiled, grunting, fiercely clinging to it.

The workers laughed. "Must be gold."

"Oh, yeah, got to be treasure."

Antonio came up beside them. "Want to keep your jobs," he said calmly, "then leave him the fuck alone and get back to work."

After they were gone, Antonio turned and walked out. He couldn't look into the man's eyes again, he realized, couldn't stand the swirling intensity. He stood in the morning sunlight and took a deep breath. He knew that look as if it were branded to the inside of his skull. He called Paolo over.

"Get one of the guys to take him away. All right? Someplace decent. But gone. I don't want to see him again."

"Understood." Paolo nodded. "*Signore Pazzo*—he is history."

ANTONIO PAUSED before the door to his father's apartment, sighed extravagantly, then knocked. He avoided Giovanni for the most part, couldn't bear his constant criticism of America, his obsession with the past. If it weren't for Sonya, he would have little to do with the man. She made all the efforts, called, sent cards on holidays. When his father contacted him, it was only to remind him to send money.

Giovanni opened the door and kissed him in the old way, on each cheek. "*Buon giorno.*"

"Morning, Papa."

"Come, Tony, sit."

Antonio settled on the sofa, the upholstery marked—by Jack—with green crayon, and spotted the first flurries of snow outside the window. He prayed it amounted to nothing. Even a few inches could bring construction to a halt.

"*Caffee?*" asked Giovanni.

"*Si, prego.*" It was an old habit, with his father, to slip into Italian; immediately he caught himself. "Please."

Giovanni brought him a cup. He seemed more fragile and decrepit than Antonio remembered. "Sonya, Jack—they are well?"

"Uh huh. Fine."

"The reason I call is . . . we have news from Sicilia . . ."

At once, Antonio rose to his feet. For weeks he had felt something building and imminent—in the world, in himself—without knowing precisely what it was. Now he knew.

"Your mother, she is dead."

III.

Antonio stood in front of a five-story apartment building, built roughly where his childhood home had once been, with small balconies and lines heavy with wet laundry. *How ugly*, he thought, *erected without any trace of imagination.* He would never have conceived of it, but he wished his father had come, after all. Despite his nostalgia, Giovanni had begged off, saying he was too old to travel. Antonio could have used the company. As he looked around, he recognized nothing from his old life. The dirt lanes—dust so bad he had had to wipe his eyes whenever a car went by—were all paved over now. And towering walls of concrete now replaced the small wooden farmhouses. The views were gone, too—rolling hills of olive trees that turned mauve at sunset. Palermo had devoured the little village and spat out a suburb.

Antonio loosened his tie, unused to the dry heat. Behind, a Vespa screamed past, causing him to cringe involuntarily. He began strolling around the building, hoping to find something he might recognize. The wake and funeral had left him surprisingly indifferent—bored, even, he was embarrassed to admit. He remembered no one—not his uncles or aunts, not cousins he had played with as a child. And his Italian was gone, as well. In rough, incomplete sentences, he stammered out the simplest information. They looked at him as if he were a fool. He was eager to be home again, back with Jack and Sonya.

He came to the rear of the building, where trash bins were lined up, and climbed the hillside. At the top, he was relieved to see a long stretch of land left undeveloped. Though he noticed his dress shoes were badly scuffed—he could picture his father shaking his head in disapproval—he continued into the dusty foothills. He still recognized nothing, felt no emotional connection. He had thought coming here would be cathartic but felt only a vague emptiness inside. He knew he should be mourning Maria, feeling guilty, perhaps, at having never visited her—or whatever she had become— while she was still alive. But that's not the way he saw it. She had already died to him when he was five.

He came to the top of a rise, where a large olive tree cast a wide shadow, and paused, out of breath, the faint smell of orange blossoms in the air. He must have scampered over these hills at some point, he thought. In the distance, a herd of goats descended into a gulley, bells clanging, then bounded up the other side. Suddenly, he recognized where he was. It had been more than forty years and yet every detail—the tree, stones, quality of the air—was charged with a kind of incandescent familiarity. He could even picture where the blade had laid at her feet.

Inadvertently, a sound rose from deep within him, a low-pitched moan, which startled him so he clasped his hands over his mouth.

IV.

Antonio climbed out of bed, unable to sleep, the house still and dark. He stepped into his slippers and cinched his robe. Perhaps it was the jetlag. Ever since returning from Italy, he had risen in the wee hours like a cat. *L'orca di nascita e morte,* he thought, astonished by how the phrase popped into his head. He walked down the hallway and paused before Jack's room, the blue nightlight leaking through beneath the door, and listened for the boy's faint breathing before continuing downstairs.

The collie lifted her head and struggled to her feet as Antonio switched on the kitchen's overhead light. She barked twice, her haunches swinging wildly with her tail. "For Christ's sake, shhh!"

Stars filled the sky, the air bitingly cold. A few inches of caked snow covered the yard, though the road and sidewalk were clear. The dog sat in the snow, leaving behind a small yellow crater.

He had blown up at work yesterday, ripped into one of the Mexicans who had dropped a bucket of nails from the second floor. It was unlike him to show any emotion at work—especially in front of the workers. Normally, every-thing went through Paolo. He had felt on edge lately, bracing himself for some indeterminate disaster.

"Relax," he told himself, a plume of steam rising from his mouth as he exhaled. He looked up into the night sky and thought how he needed to turn to something greater—not unlike his mother, really—to quell the fears. Had madness triggered her devotion or devotion her madness? He would like to have forgiven her, remembered her with compassion, filed her existence neatly away. But that was not possible. For Jack, he had to remain vigilant, watchful, prepared to fight Maria's legacy—her ghost.

The books said he had time—till adolescence. There were signs: manic swings, paranoia. Trauma could set it off like an electrical storm. Then again, there were medications now, too—miraculous stuff. Perhaps even the bagman, Jesus, could be saved.

Antonio paced along the walkway, feeling more hopeful, hands in his robe pockets, the collie snuffling at his feet. Then he noticed a pile of snow on the edge of his property. "Son of a bitch!" he said out loud, realizing his neighbor had deliberately dumped it in his yard. At once, without forethought, he marched into the snow, giddy with rage, his slippers falling away. Barefoot, cursing, he stooped and began scooping up handfuls of snow and ice then tossing them into his neighbor's yard. The dog barked, darting back and forth. His belt came undone and his robe opened. And though he dimly acknowledged the cold, the sense of absurdity, he, nevertheless, fell to his knees and became more determined, continuing until he reached the hard ground, his hands raw and throbbing.

When Antonio finally looked up, he found his wife and son, in nightclothes and slippers, standing in the doorway. Tentatively, he raised a hand, which fluttered before his eyes like a neurological event. *My God,* he thought, *what do they see if not a man cursed?* Just then, Jack tottered up to him, still groggy but smiling, grabbed a handful of snow and tossed it in the air.

French Windows

At dusk, Frank opened the windows wide to his boys' room—floor-to-ceiling windows that swung open like barn doors. A cool April wind rushed in. The view of northern Paris was disappointing: a muddle of cheap, gray apartment buildings festooned with satellite dishes, the soccer stadium, a red TOSHIBA sign, and beyond, a pink band of back-lit smog. It was an area where Arabs and Africans lived. To walk certain streets was to walk through, say, Marrakech, he imagined, though he had never been. He still couldn't get over the rent: double the mortgage of his Chicago townhouse.

His sons—Philip, aged five, and Paul, seven—jostled up against him, faces aloft, the younger boy tugging on his arm. He welcomed the contact, the heat and fervor of it, which he hadn't felt in a long time. They had his wife's eyes, he thought, like molasses. They pleaded with him to read *Lucky Luke* before bed, the forties comic strip about a fast-draw American cowboy, which still had a vibrant life in France. They pronounced it with an accent, *lewkey lewk*, puckering their mouths perversely.

He had essentially flown across the Atlantic to babysit. He was no longer allowed to ask with whom his wife had gone out, or even the gender. Such questions, they had agreed, only made things worse. Like an addict, he could barely stand being in his own skin.

She was suffocating, she said one day—*out of the fucking blue*—had fallen out of love and was moving back home to France. He could come or not; it was up to him. After thirteen years of living through and for him, as she put it, it was time to live for herself. That was seven months ago and, every month since, Frank had shuttled back and forth between O'Hare and Charles de Gaulle, determined to see his kids, to be a part of their lives. It was amazing how un-phased they were by it all, how well adapted. They had new friends now, spoke fluent French, and thought nothing of eating cheese that smelled, to Frank, like something rotten.

Frank knew this arrangement—him flying back and forth for long weekends—couldn't last. He had already burned through their savings and was up to his eyeballs in debt. Plus, with the recession and all the time off, could he realistically hope to keep his job at TMP? The place was already crawling with copywriters and there had been murmurs of layoffs.

He told the boys that if they quieted down and got into bed he'd read to them. Though, as the warmth of them receded, he was sorry to have said it.

He leaned out the window, his pelvis pressing against the low railing, and reached for the wooden shutters, arms spread wide as if on the verge of flight. The shutters rested against the outside wall, a small latch holding them in place. While one gave easily, turning on its hinges, the other remained stuck. He leaned farther out, taking the shutter more firmly in hand. Strips of gray paint, decades-old, flecked off and fell to the courtyard below. He paused and watched their descent, like butterflies, and found himself slipping into a distant, fugue-like state in which everything seemed slightly unreal. The space before him suddenly charged with infinite promise. How simple and stunning, he thought—an alternative he had never considered before—like plunging into the sea. He imagined it: the sudden freedom and release. The blackening of his soul wiped clean. As he hung there, prone, six floors up, he thought: *Let go . . .*

For the time being, though, he didn't let go. He stared down at the courtyard, as if into a well, and envisioned, with surprising clarity and detachment, falling through liquid space, which he imagined as utterly still and outside of time. He wondered briefly if it was high enough. Then he considered the impact, so startlingly abrupt and nullifying. *And then what?* As his mind wrestled with this last imponderable, his wife must have walked in, because the boys erupted with, "*Maman, Maman...*" He couldn't distinguish her words, only the cadence and timber of her voice, though even this seemed to threaten him. To face her now would be a kind of annihilation.

He looked out over northern Paris, the light dropping off. *The blue hour,* they called it. Then he spotted an Arab woman, middle-aged, standing in a fifth-floor window in the building opposite him, about thirty yards away. She was smoking a cigarette and regarding him coolly, as if she had been through worse and was unimpressed. She acknowledged him with a slight nod, exhaling a stream of smoke, and Frank nodded back.

A moment later he felt his wife's hand on the small of his back. "Frank?"

The effect was devastating. *For Christ's sake,* he thought, *don't cry,* keeping his face turned from her. "Shutter's stuck," he said at last.

"*Attention . . .*" she said and grabbed him by the waist. "Try lifting it." Then she must have felt something strange in the way he held himself. "Frank . . ." she said, "it's going to be all right—*vraiment.*"

He pictured her lips, the curious swell and curve of them, which he had first adored, her crooked smile.

"You're going to be okay."

He recognized her perfume: jasmine and rose, a hint of musk. He would have to sell the townhouse, resign himself to seeing the boys over holidays. It would be a long time before he was okay again.

The woman across the way tossed her cigarette into the expanse of the courtyard—sparks trailing behind—then closed her window. In what passed as an instant, night slipped over the city like a formal gown. From behind, his sons clamored for *Lucky Luke*, and he knew he had no choice but to throw himself into the vast and terrifying moment before him.

When he pulled on the shutter, it swung free and slammed against the window frame with a loud bang like a gunshot.

Shooting with Helmut

The morning you fly from Paris to Monte Carlo to meet Helmut Newton you have a cold and feel like hell. As you pull up in front of the Hermitage Hotel, where Newton makes his home, the taxi driver asks if you would like a prostitute for the evening. His offer comes as a shock and seems out of character with your lavish surroundings, but then you realize that this is a place where people spare nothing to get what they want. "*Non merci,*" you say. Everything about Monte Carlo is dazzling and expensive-looking—the streets, homes, cars, gardens. Everything looks freshly washed and meticulously cared for. And, filtering down from above, the Mediterranean sun bathes it all in a pinkish, crystalline light, as if shot through a diamond.

You give your name at the front desk. "Monsieur Newton is expecting you," says the concierge. As you stand in the antique elevator, rising to the top floor, you think of his indelible images—long-legged, big-breasted women, powerful, erotic, unapproachable, often wearing nothing but high heels, vaguely sadistic. He is one of your heroes, someone who has devoted his entire life to expressing his fantasies without compromise.

Your all-too-cool agency in Paris had called with uncharacteristic enthusiasm. "Newton wants to see you!" Normally, Newton only booked women, never men. It was like being summoned by the king. Even Lindbergh, Weber, and Ritts labored in his shadow. He was beyond needing clients, accolades, or compensation. In the fashion world, it was not too much to say that a Newton project was like a revelation; it would alter the course of the industry.

You call Paris home, though you live out of a suitcase most of the time. Your suburban American past seems like a distant incarnation. Paris is where your mother agency is, where your girlfriend is, and where you need to live in order to command a Parisian model rate. You are nearly thirty and have been modeling for five years—despite your family's reservations—and are on the verge of breaking into the big leagues. And you know that working with Newton would put you decisively there.

A young, muscular girl dressed in shorts, boots, and a white tank top greets you at the door, her blond hair pulled taut into a ponytail. She leads you to a sitting room filled with books, antiques, large black-and-white details of women's bodies. "Do you have your book with you?" she asks with a German accent. You hand her your modeling book. She flips through it rapidly. "Take a seat," she says and disappears. You imagine her showing it to Helmut and then Helmut summoning you. And though you know it's ridiculous, you can't help but be thrilled at the prospect of meeting the man. You begin to cough, then sneeze, phlegm rattling in your chest—infuriated that on this day of all days you should be sick. From the sitting room you see an older woman, dark-haired, with bangs, sunbathing on the porch and, beyond, a line of palms and the deep blue of the Mediterranean.

You hear what you assume is Helmut laughing. Is it your book he's laughing at? After a while the girl reappears. "Helmut is busy," she says, "but June will see you."

Crestfallen, you figure you have just been blown off. You follow the girl out onto the porch, where the actress June Browne (a.k.a. Brunell)—Newton's wife and muse, and the subject of countless photo studies—reclines in a black bikini. Though in her sixties, she looks years younger. You introduce yourself, tell her you're American and, when not modeling, a poet. She raises her sunglasses, looks you over. She lights a cigarette and smiles. "Well, James," she says, "we look forward to seeing you in L.A."

A MONTH LATER, you arrive in Los Angeles. They put you up at Chateau Marmont, where Helmut keeps a suite year-round, known for its ambiance of excess and as the hotel where John Belushi overdosed. It's elegantly rundown, tucked away in a grove of palms, with a nice view of the city from your balcony. Models, stylists, hair and makeup artists fly in from all corners of the globe. No one knows the concept of the shoot, not even the client. All you know is that you are shooting a campaign for an Italian fashion designer, though the client is immaterial. It's obvious that the shoot is only an opportunity, an excuse really, for Newton to live out his latest fantasy.

The first few days you only have fittings to go to and spend your time by the pool reading and spotting movie stars. You still haven't actually met Helmut, though you have been studying his images, trying to prepare yourself, imagining the hour when you stand face to face with his lens.

You see June one morning in the hotel lobby, wearing sunglasses, heels, an elegant black suit. You greet one another French-style, pecking each other on the cheek. "Why are you alone?" she says, concerned. "Such a handsome man shouldn't be alone—not in L.A . . . Gracious, do I need to fix you up with someone?"

"No, no, I'm fine," you say.

"Sweetie, you don't understand . . . You are in L.A. What cars are to Detroit, young, beautiful, single women are to L.A. Go have some fun."

That night you go out with two girls from the shoot, C. and E., both of whom happen to be deemed supermodels. Every once in a while, C. tosses her long blond hair, flashes her breathtaking smile, and E. sinuously dips a shoulder, cocks a hip, looks at you with her dark, bedroom eyes, and you see why they are so sought after, paid so much. Wherever you go, first a restaurant, later a disco, people appear stupefied, staring and hovering at the periphery, as if struck by some neurological disorder. At first, you get a kick out of being seen with them, but very soon the constant scrutiny grows unbearable. You realize even your greatest dreams of success are insignificant compared to the realm in which they reside. No one dares approach the girls or speak to them. Even talking is awkward as every word that passes between you is overheard by strangers. It becomes impossible to relax.

"My God," you say as you sit in the disco's VIP lounge, "how do you stand it?"

"Stand what?" says C., shouting over the pulsing music.

"All this attention!"

They laugh. "This is nothing compared to when I'm out with Steven," says E., referring to her rock star boyfriend.

"Yeah," says C., who won't even mention her boyfriend's name, "it can get really crazy."

So here you are, experiencing the overspill of fame—which, as they explain it, is nothing compared to their boyfriends' fame—and yet even this is far more than anything you can stand. You think of all the people who long for fame as if it were the height of aspiration. But to experience even an hour of such notoriety would leave almost anyone reeling, desperate to have their anonymity restored.

E. grabs you by the hand and pulls you to your feet. "I feel like moving," she says, and it's clear she's someone accustomed to getting what she wants. You dance a few songs together. She moves languidly like a bored cat. You think of that music video in which she rolls on the beach in a bikini—sand powdering her olive skin like sugar—and the singer fondles her while she looks at her nails. You imagine her being impossible to satisfy.

Later, back at the hotel, you and E. sit alone at the bar for a nightcap. You have the insatiable desire to reach out and touch her, like that singer in the video, only you can't shake the thought that this is E., the face (and body) of L'Oréal, Victoria's Secret . . .

June walks in and sits down next to you. "So?" she says. "Happy now? Does Auntie June know best?" You have no idea what she's talking about. She nods toward E. in a knowing sort of way. And suddenly it dawns on you that it was June who had arranged the evening, who had convinced C. and E. to ask you out in the first place. She lights a cigarette. "So much beauty . . ." she says of E. "How in the world can you resist?"

E. rolls her eyes. "She's trying to fix us up . . . in case you were wondering."

"Ah," you say. Though you had figured E. was out of bounds, out of your league—the inamorata of a rock star.

June gets to her feet. "Do not ignore what the gods hath wrought. . ." she says with a smile. "Goodnight, my dears."

The next morning, as you lie in bed next to E., she confesses that she feels so incredibly alone and isolated. She had clung to you half the night as if she might drown or fall from a great height.

"Sometimes," she says, "I feel like everyone is looking at me like I'm deformed or something."

SHE STUFFS HER HAIR in a cap, puts on baggy sweats, sneakers, sunglasses—"my schlepping clothes," she says—and still people recognize her. You note the frequent double takes as you stroll along Venice Beach. A pack of rollerbladers streaks past. It's morning and already the sun scorches your shoulders, the top of your head. An elderly black woman says you make an adorable couple. E. smiles and takes your hand, swinging it back and forth, like you're a couple of teenagers walking down the halls of junior high.

"So, where's Steven?" you ask, his name dropping like a stone between you.

"On tour," she says, looking away, "in Europe somewhere . . . Milan, I think."

You walk for a while, still holding hands. You seem to share the same guiltless, fluid sense of what a relationship can be in this business. You pass a vendor, enveloped in steam that smells of hot dogs.

"He's probably with someone as I speak," she says.

You notice the crowds milling by—so many transparent faces. It's a cruel vision, but this is how the industry has formed you: anyone whose appearance is less than extraordinary you automatically disregard.

You stop and buy her an ice cream cone, which she licks as if it were a magnificent art. You continue down the boardwalk, passing a fortune-teller in a turban, a guy on acoustic guitar playing bad Dylan. She tells you about the small Scandinavian village where she grew up, about her beloved *mormor* and ice skating and eating pickled herring on rye.

You pause to watch the weightlifters at Muscle Beach, as they make their masochistic sounds, plates clanging together, bodies like overstuffed sofas—as if you're watching an alien species on display. One of them recognizes E. You can see it by the way he keeps looking at her, sweeping back his bleached hair, adjusting his crotch. He turns to another bodybuilder, a black guy with dreadlocks, and points to her. In unison, they call out her name. You perceive others turning, recognizing her. The weightlifters draw closer, flexing their muscles, laughing, asking if E. would like to touch. You stand motionless together as the rank smell of their sweat surrounds you. You sense their steroid-laden bodies brimming with barely contained aggression.

"What are you doing with this skinny pretty boy?" asks the one with bleached hair. It feels like half of Venice is watching.

She turns to you with panic in her eyes, then looks down at her sneakers. "Take me away from here, please."

AT DAWN, A LOCATION van drives you north of Malibu to a grassy bluff high above the Pacific, a glow building in the hills to the east. The air smells clean and salty and of seaweed. Already a half-dozen trucks have gathered in the twilight. An army of workers scurries about setting up tables, chairs, racks of clothes, movie lights, generators humming.

The Italian designer rises from his lounge chair to greet C. and E., giggling with uncontainable enthusiasm (you, he almost entirely ignores). He looks like a wax figure, with his jet-black toupee, impeccable tan, tautly renovated features. "*Molto bella!*" he says of the girls. "*Bellisima!*" His entourage eagerly agrees: "*Si, bellisima!*" The art director, another gay Italian man, dressed in a rose-colored suit, explains the premise of the shoot, which, as he points out, can change at a moment's notice depending upon the whims of Signore Newton: "There is a wedding party," he says. "And you may or may not be the groom . . . Or maybe it is just a party . . ."

Now that you are finally on the verge of shooting with Helmut, you feel jittery and self-conscious. They dress you up in a tuxedo, blow dry your hair into a duck's wedge. The girls put on long, sequined gowns that look sprayed on, their hair mounted in elaborate buns. You are told not to sit down, for fear of wrinkling your clothes, though the girls collapse almost immediately.

A long, elegantly set table stands at the center of the meadow, draped in a pristine white tablecloth. A string quartet sits before their instruments in evening gowns and black tie. Everyone is waiting. Though no one has seen or heard from Helmut. Even his photo-assistants have no idea where he could be, explaining to the designer that Mister Newton is probably just waiting for the right light. "I do not wait," says the designer. As the day wears on, he grows more and more irate, lashing out at his entourage in vehement Italian.

The sun beats down from directly overhead. A general malaise settles over the crew. E., perhaps bored, leads you behind a catering truck and French kisses you till your knees go wobbly. By afternoon, one of Helmut's assistants receives a call and reports that Mister Newton is about to leave L.A.; he has just one more thing to take care of. . . .

An hour goes by, then another. C. and E. persuade the caterers to break out the caviar and champagne (intended as photo-props). And soon the string quartet, at the girls' request, launches into Mozart. Amazing what a pair of super-models can get people to do. A breeze picks up off the Pacific. The sun tumbles over the bay in a blazing arc. After working himself up into such a state, the designer has fallen asleep beneath a beach umbrella.

You hear the helicopter before you see it. Then it appears to the south, moving toward you along the coast, sweeping in fast. The crew goes quiet and collectively turns. Before long, it hovers just above you, maybe thirty feet off the ground. You assume it will begin to descend, but, instead, it simply hangs there as if by a chord. Meanwhile, violent, swirling gusts from the propeller blades upend chairs, clothes racks, a movie light—which appears to explode as it hits the ground. Sand and bits of grass fly up into your face. Dresses, suits, overcoats shake off their hangers, sail across the bluff and vanish over the cliff's edge, like a procession of martyrs hurling themselves without hesitation to their deaths. Tablecloths rise and fill with air, tossing plates and glasses—scattering silverware like pick-up sticks. C. and E.'s perfectly coiffed hair instantly turns frizzy and lopsided. Their skirts billow up around them like Marilyn Monroe's in *The Seven Year Itch*—revealing their delicate under things. Everyone is in a state of motion, chasing all manner of flying, cartwheeling things. And looking utterly bewildered, the designer stands there watching his beach umbrella capsize and scud away.

Then you spot Helmut, leaning out of the helicopter with camera in hand, and immediately recognize the floppy hair and bulbous nose, the eternally boyish, handsome face. You see him firing away—something almost fanatical about his concentration—filling one roll after another, pausing only to grab a fresh camera.

A moment or two goes by like this and, when it is clear that the helicopter will not be landing, the designer succumbs to a paroxysm of rage, shouting and stomping his feet and stabbing his hands into the air.

Then it comes to you, with absolute certainty: the photos will be extraordinary, a tremendous success, worth every penny—a brilliant, deconstructive, self-mocking take on haute couture. You can even imagine the designer declaring himself a genius for giving Helmut free rein.

For an instant, Helmut seems to be looking directly at you from the cockpit, with a broad smile, as if this is all a priceless, private joke between you. Without fully realizing it, you find yourself smiling back. It would be the first and last time you see Helmut Newton.

A moment later, the helicopter turns and speeds down the coast toward L.A., soon vanishing around a bend in the shoreline.

YEARS LATER, you read of Helmut's death in *The Herald Tribune*, how he sped from Chateau Marmont one night and smashed his car into the front gate, instantly killing himself (another footnote in the hotel's salacious history). And though you will never see June again, she sends a postcard one year from Monte Carlo, inquiring about your love life, closing with, *Love, Auntie June*. In the end, you will have your success—a few years of stardom. But, like everything in this business, nothing lasts.

You see E. one more time in the early 90s, during show season in Paris, on Place de la Concorde. She is just stepping out of a taxi with her new boyfriend, the famous French tennis star. She wears a short skirt and boots, her rich brown hair shorter, fashionably disheveled. She is decisively on, in full supermodel mode, strutting down the sidewalk, apparently at ease now in her celebrity roll. From across the intersection, you call her name. She turns and looks, first one way then the other, unable to place the voice. And for a fleeting instant, you see the vulnerable girl who clung to you half the night. Then, taking the tennis star by the hand, she continues along Rue Royale, into the growing swell of admirers.

Lan and Jin

Every few months I left Tokyo for Hong Kong to renew my visa. I usually stayed about a week and always in the same place—a tiny hostel on the 26th floor of a high rise. The ceilings were so low that to enter the hostel, stepping out of the elevator, I had to duck my head. The rooms were miniscule, more like closets really, with just enough room for a single bed and sink—too small even to do a push-up. The views, though, were magnificent, especially at night, when the city ignited with garish brand names, looking festive and trashy and futuristic, like a scene out of *Blade Runner*.

At night, I strolled through the carnival-like streets, the outdoor markets and endless shopping malls strung along the harbor, studying faces, feeling isolated and alone, longing to descend beneath the city's frenetic surface and connect— with what or whom I couldn't say.

Days I ran up Victoria Peak, following the narrow, winding lane, with thick, nearly tropical vegetation on one side, the city and bay falling away on the other, and an endless string of automobiles streaming past. I needed the challenge, to turn myself inside out, and climbed at race tempo for an hour or more—T-shirt sopping, calves burning, gulping exhaust—as if back in college again running cross country.

Once I reached the summit I collapsed onto a bench, spent, and stared down at the city, where toy junks drifted across Victoria Harbor, light slid over towering steel-and-glass façades, and millions scurried like insects. I felt utterly blank—the world at once removed and within my grasp, as if reality could be altered by will alone. It had been two years since I left the States in the wake of my father's death, and I longed to do something exceptional—write, be a jazz musician. At twenty-three, nothing seemed more valuable than being an artist. A fashion model—certainly that wasn't me.

Eventually, I would take the tram down the mountain and return to my little room, feeling dreamy and full of wild impulses, all the while stringing sentences together which sounded gorgeous in the cathedral of my mind. But as soon as I set them down on paper, they looked phony and ridiculous.

Of course, the only reason for adopting my Hong Kong regime was to stave off having to confront myself. The idea of facing the big question—*What are you doing with your life?*—was to fall into an unimaginable void.

One day, after running up Victoria Peak, I met a Chinese couple coming down on the tram. They were in their thirties, attractive, impeccably dressed, spoke with an English accent. *Had I run up the peak?* they asked. *I had,* I said. They made big eyes. The woman said something in Chinese to her husband. He nodded. A moment later, she said, "You look like a young Kennedy."

I smiled. I had heard it before but didn't know how to respond.

They asked where I was from, what I was doing there. *Boston,* I lied, *I'm on holiday.* I couldn't bring myself to tell them I was a model, without a real home, an opportunist capitalizing on my looks—my Kennedy-like looks—and exploiting the Japanese and their ripe economy.

They asked me to join them for dinner. They would send a car. At six that evening, a limousine pulled up in front of my building, a jet-black Bentley. The driver, a grim-looking

Chinese fellow who wore black leather gloves, didn't say a word except to ask my name. About an hour later, after driving south across Hong Kong Island to the seaside village of Stanley, he climbed a steep, single lane through dense jungle and turned into a driveway. He parked below the house, which was built high up into the hillside and spectacularly lit. We took a small, creaking elevator, which looked like it belonged in a Parisian apartment building, up through the bowels of the mountain. When it stopped and the elevator doors slid open, I had the sensation of being transported to an alternate reality. Everything glowed supernaturally and ripples of light played over the walls and ceiling as if I were within an ocean grotto. The immediate room appeared staid and colonial—oriental rugs, wood-paneling—but then, down a short staircase, the house opened onto a patio and swimming pool, and beyond, the Po Toi Islands and South China Sea.

The driver withdrew, descending in the elevator, and a Chinese woman, dressed in a French maid's uniform, led me to the patio, took my drink order and disappeared. High above, palm fronds shifted against the sky. The sun was setting and I stood at the railing watching the bay turn a deep crimson that made me think of a massacre at sea.

"Ah, there you are." The hostess appeared, dressed in a sleek, plum-colored evening gown with plunging décolleté, her hair pulled back, feet bare. She wore pearls and smoked from a long, ivory cigarette holder. As she kissed me lightly on each cheek, I took in her scent: citrus and rose, tobacco, a hint of perspiration. "I hope you're hungry," she said.

The maid returned and handed me a glass of *Yanjing*. Behind her the host arrived, bowing ceremoniously, wearing black tie. In my wrinkled linens, I felt ridiculously underdressed.

"James, welcome," he said. I felt at a distinct disadvantage, not recalling either of their names. We settled into wicker chairs, which creaked beneath us with every shift of weight.

At a corner of the patio, in a large cage, a pair of parrots repeated the same Chinese phrase over and over again.

"What are they saying?" I asked.

"Oh, nothing," he said. "Nonsense."

"He just doesn't want to tell you," she said, laughing. "Jin curses like a sailor."

"I do not," he said.

"Oh, please—you most certainly do."

The host sighed. "To be precise, the phrase is *Qing wa cao de liu mang*, which means, *Frog-humping son-of-a-bitch* . . . You see, I often pace out here when I make business calls, which may explain the colorful language."

We all laughed.

The maid came with more drinks. Night fell. A warm breeze blew in off the sea. I discovered the hostess's name—Lan—and admired the slender line of her body, the way she sat with her legs folded beneath her, the arch of her back. In the distance, across the straits, a suburb blazed like a galaxy.

We went in for dinner. There were candles, a white tablecloth, a French Merlot. We started with vichyssoise, moved on to watercress salad, then braised endives and *bœuf bourguignon*, and ended with *crème brûlée*—everything superb.

They spoke together in Chinese, and Jin's face subtly changed as if he had swallowed something distasteful.

I raised my glass of Merlot and complimented them on their hospitality, the meal, their exquisite home.

"Our pleasure," Lan said.

"Yes," said Jin, though he seemed distracted. A moment later, tugging on his shirt cuffs, he took on a confidential tone: "Forgive me, James, but then I am just a businessman, and not nearly as sophisticated as my dear wife . . ." He said this with palpable sarcasm. "I think it's about time we spoke up and did away with all the subterfuge . . ."

Lan clucked her tongue. "Jin!"

"Ah, you see, my wife wants romance, spontaneity, nothing as crass as a proposition."

As she lit her cigarette, the ivory holder trembled in her hand.

"I'm sure, from the way Lan has conducted herself this evening, it comes as no surprise that she wants to sleep with you."

Lan turned her face violently away, exhaling a stream of smoke. Too embarrassed to look him in the eye, I stared into my wineglass.

"And, naturally, a man wants to please his wife—no? But, alas, there's no graceful way to overcome jealousy—all that petit-bourgeois hysteria . . ." He downed his glass. "So, tell me, James . . . do you find my wife attractive?"

I hesitated. "Very pretty," I said.

"Pretty!"

"Oh, stop bullying him, Jin!"

"But, my dear, I'm only inquiring if he's up to the task."

"Maybe I should go," I said, starting to rise.

"You see," she said, "you're scaring him away. . ."

"Oh, for God's sake, do sit down."

She turned to me, her eyes heartbreakingly sad. "Please excuse my husband . . ."

I hovered a moment longer before sitting down again.

"Jin, make amends."

"Certainly, by all means . . ." He smoothed his hair. "If I've acted like an ass—which seems to be my tendency these days—I do apologize." He said this to no one in particular.

Lan then rang a small, golden bell, summoning the maid. "Shall we take our drinks on the patio? Such a lovely evening . . ."

We returned to the wicker chairs; the parrots resumed their chanting. Spotlights lit up the treetops. The Jacuzzi mysteriously gurgled to life. The maid brought cognacs. On the table before us lay a mirror with six neatly drawn lines of cocaine on it, and a small silver tube.

Before long, Jin leaned forward, matter-of-factly, and snorted up two lines in quick succession, then, pinching his nose, settled back into his chair with a satisfied grin.

Lan then positioned the mirror in front of me. "Please," she said, "help yourself."

I had tried coke before, and liked its effects, but usually begged off—imagining myself in training. *But what the hell,* I thought, *the evening held untold possibilities.* I took up the silver tube, ducked my head, and snorted up a line, then, reeling a little, collapsed into the wicker chair.

Lan took her turn, devouring the coke with relish, then stood, walked over to the Jacuzzi with cognac in hand, and stripped off her clothes, pearls and underwear. She lowered herself into the bubbling water, her body as delicate as a child's.

"No time to be shy," said Jin, rising from his chair.

Soon we were all in the water together, naked, drinking cognacs and laughing. From the coke, I felt jazzed up and infallible. Someone brushed a foot against my thigh. The thought that it might be Jin, hankering for a threesome, triggered a rush of homoerotic fears and I pulled away.

Moments later, Lan said something in Chinese to Jin, at which point he stood from the water, penis dangling, and bowed in the same ceremonious way he had greeted me. "Farewell, young Kennedy." Then, to his wife, he said: "May your night be divine"—having apparently suppressed or transcended his jealousy.

Once he had gone, Lan and I faced each other, motionless. Then, beneath the churning surface, I felt her hand slide up my leg.

When we had finished, she kissed me tenderly, lingering a beat, then excused herself. I assumed she would be right back, had only gone to the bathroom. But then minutes passed, and I realized she wasn't coming back.

Eventually, the chauffeur tapped me on the shoulder. It must have been close to midnight. I dressed and followed him back to the elevator and down to the car. He drove in silence along the coast, the sea dark and rolling, the rim of the sky glowing faintly from city lights. I had come down hard from the cocaine. Moments, impressions, repeated themselves: the dinner and Jin's thinly concealed rage, the cocaine and Jacuzzi, the blissful pain of release, the parrots screeching, and Lan's sad eyes.

Back in the city, a delivery truck blocked my street, which was still animated despite the hour, and the Bentley stopped at the corner. I thanked the driver and stepped out. When I slammed the door, he sped off without any acknowledgement.

I found myself standing in front of a restaurant. Behind its front window, a half-dozen snakes writhed within a large glass bowl, slithering up the bowl's steep sides, under and over each other, repeatedly, pointlessly—only to slide back down again. One—jet-black with orange piping and a flanged head—struck at the others with startling ferocity. I stood there, stunned, a little queasy, as if watching a detail come to life from Rodin's *The Gates of Hell*.

An old Chinese man lingered beside me, wearing a tra-ditional, black Chinese suit. He laughed, observing my expression, and smacked his lips as if relishing the taste of snake. I nodded, pretended to smile, then turned to face myself in the window.

Mejdoub

Here in this wholly mineral landscape lighted by stars like flares, even memory disappears . . .

A strange, and by no means pleasant, process of reintegration begins inside you . . .

For no one who has stayed in the Sahara for a while is quite the same as when he came.

—Paul Bowles

I.

As twilight fell, they wound their way out of the Atlas Mountains down to the desert floor, passing medieval villages built directly into the mountainside, waterfalls that plunged thousands of feet. They opened the windows wide and let the warm desert wind pour into the car. The air smelled of orange blossoms and dung. Simon welcomed the small grains of sand that collected in the corners of his eyes. He felt relaxed. Everything seemed different now that they were at the edge of the desert.

They stopped for gas, nuts and dates, a case of bottled water. They drove on in the darkness. Elisabeth curled up and laid her head in his lap. The pale green light of the dash lit her face.

"*Ça va?* So you are happy now?" she said.

"Yes."

"*Bien.*" She closed her eyes. Soon she was snoring softly.

The road was empty, the stars and headlights his only light. He pulled over to the side of the road and eased Elisabeth's head off his lap onto the seat. He got out of the car, a bottle of J&B in hand. He stared out into the rich blackness. Far off, he could hear bells clanging—goats or cows or maybe camels—the air turning cold. The sense of being isolated and alone pressed in from all sides. Simon climbed up on the hood of the car and lay back with his hands behind his head, enjoying the warmth of the engine ticking beneath him. He stared up at the desert sky, ink-black and swirling with starlight. He felt light years from everything, on the verge of a new incarnation.

He had no idea where his ex-wife was or who she was with. He had shut his ears to the rumors, sold everything— the house, stocks, cars, business, then split it all down the middle. He would put it all behind him now, start over again.

He took another gulp of whiskey, relishing the slow burn, and turned to check on Elisabeth through the window. She was sleeping soundly, hands between her legs, eyes fluttering, lost in a dream. Roughly half his age, she was often mistaken for his daughter. She wore torn jeans, a T-shirt, had a tattoo of a scorpion on her shoulder. Her hair was thick and black and often hung in her face. Wherever they went men stared at her.

He remembered the first time he saw her in Paris, dancing with her girlfriend at Les Bains. In the subdued lighting, she looked vaguely like his ex-wife, only a younger version. He was bumbling and tongue-tied, but she seemed to find it endearing. They met the next day for lunch and the day after that. Soon they were spending whole afternoons together in his hotel room.

He stood, stretched, and took a long deep breath, reeling slightly from the whiskey, then got back into the car, gently lifting Elisabeth's head and returning it to his lap.

Tomorrow, he was sure, the desert would begin to remake him.

Simon continued south toward Ouarzazate. The guidebook advertised it as the location of *Lawrence of Arabia*. As he strained to recall the film, all he could picture was Peter O'Toole's impassioned face—gaunt and artificially tan. As he came within a few kilometers of town, he could already see it, blazing with streetlights. The road abruptly changed from a bumpy, barely paved single lane into a sleek, ultra-modern four lane highway, though his was still the only car on the road. As he idled into town, Simon noticed clean, whitewashed buildings with strategically placed dramatic lighting, as if he had entered a movie set. Everything appeared groomed and modernized to impress tourists. Simon was disappointed. He had expected a sleepy desert outpost—not this.

He took another draught of whiskey and settled on a hotel in what looked to be the old part of town, near the *souqs*, then woke Elisabeth. As they entered the lobby, Simon immediately wanted to leave. It was altogether too much—the white marble, red carpeting, gold railings. He had hoped for something more modest and authentic, even a little squalid.

"Let's go. We'll find another hotel."

"What are you talking about?"

"I don't like it."

"*Mon amour*, I need a bath. We need to eat. *C'est bon*."

He relented, realizing at once he was too drunk and tired to do otherwise. They checked in and took dinner in their room. The *tajine* tasted rancid. He took a few bites and climbed into bed, not bothering to bathe. He drifted off to sleep, then woke sometime later to Elisabeth climbing into bed, her hair still wet, smelling of watermelon and wildflowers. She kissed him gently, pressed herself naked against him. Soon she was above him, straddling him. As much as he tried to respond, there was nothing.

"Elisabeth . . . Elisabeth."

Gradually, she came to a halt.

"Sorry, I can't. I just can't. It's not in me tonight."

"*T'es chiant!*" She swung off him in a fury, exhaling sharply, and retreated to the far side of the bed.

"I drank too much. It's not you."

She sat up, raging, hair wild. "*Mais t'es pire qu'un vieux schnok! Pauvre minable, espèce de grand 'Ricain débile, va!*"

He had no idea what she said, but decided that was probably a good thing. She rolled away, snapping the sheet up and over her. He tried to stroke her hip to console her, but she swatted his hand away as if it were a mosquito.

The next morning, they set off early. Simon's head ached and his mouth tasted vile. Still, hangover or no hangover, he wanted to leave Ouarzazate behind, find a place untarnished by tourism. The air-conditioning gave out after an hour on the road. As they opened the windows, a hellish wind filled the car. There was nowhere to look, no escape from the light. The sun filled every corner of the sky. The land was flat and featureless—nothing but sunbaked gravel and small thorny trees. As Simon drank his whiskey, hoping to improve his state, Elisabeth smoked steadily and avoided looking him in the eye.

Up ahead they spotted a car on the side of the road and two young Moroccan men waving them down.

Elisabeth turned to him. "I hope you're going to stop."

"I don't think it's a good idea."

"Oh, Simon, you must. What if it were us?"

"All right . . . but, for the record, I still think it's a bad idea."

He pulled up behind the other car and got out. The two Moroccans came toward him, smiling, talking excitedly in French. Their teeth appeared unnaturally white.

"Sorry, I don't speak French."

"*Pas de français?*" said the taller of the two. "*Allemand?*"

"No. American."

They looked at one another. Although he saw nothing in their expressions, Simon knew most Moroccans vilified Americans.

"Hold on." He turned and waved to Elisabeth, motioning her forward. She got out of the car, dropped her cigarette to the pavement and ground it out with the heel of her shoe. As she made her way toward them, the Moroccans seemed to shift anxiously, speaking in soft conspiratorial tones. The shorter of the two let out a brief, surprisingly high-pitched laugh, then stopped himself.

Elisabeth struck a pose of indifference, cocking her hip to one side, looking off into the distance, lifting the weight of her hair off the back of her neck then letting it fall again.

The Moroccans looked mesmerized.

The taller one spoke: "*Madame, notre voiture . . .*"

"*Mademoiselle,*" she said, correcting him.

"*Ah, oui, bien sûr. . . .*" He went on in rapid-fire French.

Elisabeth turned to Simon. "Their car is dead. He says he needs a ride to Zagora."

"What about the other one?"

"He says his cousin will stay behind and watch the car."

Briefly, the two Moroccans bickered in Arabic. Then the taller of the two handed the shorter one a small pile of dirham, at which point they both seemed satisfied.

There was roughly an hour to go still before they reached Zagora. It was ten in the morning though the heat was already devastating. The Moroccan, who had introduced himself as Belqassim, sat mutely in back. A sweet, musky odor emanated from him. Simon felt like having another shot of whiskey but didn't want to offend the Muslim. He drank from the water bottle instead. Elisabeth inserted one of her French dance tapes into the tape player and turned up the volume. Here we go again, Simon thought, rolling his eyes. At once, the young Moroccan leaned forward, thrusting his head between them.

"*C'est MC Solaar, non? J'adore MC Solaar!*"

"*Oui!*" Elisabeth lit up with enthusiasm. "*Vous connaissez MC Solaar?*"

"*Bien sûr*," he said, nodding and grinning.

She looked at Simon. "You see, Simon, I am not alone. Belqassim also likes my music. He has taste. He likes MC Solaar."

"How wonderful," Simon said.

They went on in this way, the Moroccan and Elisabeth, finding, like touchstones, common points of reference from pop culture. At one point, even with his rudimentary grasp of the language, Simon noticed a sudden, mutual shift in their conversation—a change from *vous* to *tu*. Turning, he briefly studied the side of the young man's face. He looked to be about twenty-five with long eyelashes, a sprinkling of pock marks, and long sideburns. The Moroccan turned to him and suddenly their faces were inches apart. Simon could smell lamb on his breath, see the delicate explosion of blood vessels in his eyes. His smile appeared, widening grotesquely, his teeth like tiny, polished headstones. Simon recoiled, grinning awkwardly, and returned his attention to the road.

In the distance, Simon spotted what looked to be an oasis—a refuge of lush palms in the middle of the desert.

"*Voilà Zagora*," said the young Moroccan.

"That's Zagora, Simon. *C'est magique, non?*"

Simon nodded, beginning to get excited. It did look magical, like something out of *The Thousand and One Nights*.

"*C'est ma ville*," said the Moroccan.

"*Vraiment?*" she said. Then to Simon she said, "He's from here. Maybe he can show us around."

"Hmmm," said Simon, realizing he desperately needed a drink.

They rolled slowly into the village, down a dusty single lane, the buildings stained red and built low to the ground. On either side, narrow alleys disappeared into the palmery. After a minute or two, they came to a small cul-de-sac, marking the end of the village. From this point onward only camels ventured. As Simon began to turn the car around, he noticed a faded sign at the side of the road with an arrow pointing into the desert. He could hardly believe what he was seeing. He stopped the car and, squinting, stared at the sign as if in a trance: *Tombouctou, 52 jours.*

BELQASSIM RECOMMENDED a small guesthouse, belonging to his uncle, on the north side of the village. He guaranteed a special price. The room was dark and bare, with two single beds and a window the size of a shoebox. The bathroom consisted of a spigot, a hole in the ground for a toilet, and a bucket—everything spotless.

"It's perfect," said Simon.

Elisabeth shook her head in disbelief and laughed. "*Simon, c'est tout un poème.*"

The next morning Belqassim arrived early as arranged and led them through the maze of the palmery. Sparrows by the thousands wheeled overhead. They watched as small boys—pollinators—scrambled up the trunks as nimbly as rats. One of the boys brought them a sparrow cupped in his hands. Simon watched in horror as the boy then crushed it, flattening it like a butterfly, and offered it to Elisabeth.

"*Ahh! C'est immonde.*" She turned away in disgust.

Belqassim laughed, barked something in Arabic at the boy, then waved him away.

The boy, clearly upset, no doubt expecting money, threw the bird to the ground and strode off.

They continued on to the market, the smells overpowering. Simon nearly gagged as they passed the spice *souq*, while Elisabeth pointed her camera at the vibrant piles of cinnamon, mustard, and paprika. Out of the corner of his eye, Simon spotted a European couple being led by Belqassim's cousin, the same fellow they had seen the day before by the side of the road. Simon watched as Belqassim and his cousin made brief eye-contact, then quickly looked away. The cousin—though Simon doubted if he really was a cousin—immediately steered the European couple to another part of the *souqs*. Simon began to wonder if their breakdown yesterday wasn't just a ploy to lure unsuspecting tourists. They seemed so clearly in cahoots.

"Elisabeth."

"*Oui?*"

"I think Belqassim's up to no good."

"Oh, Simon, please."

"I'm serious."

"Simon, there's no grand conspiracy here. He makes a little money, we get a tour. *C'est tout.*"

Later, Belqassim invited them for tea at the shop of one of his cousins.

"Another cousin," Simon mumbled. "Is there anybody he's not related to?"

"Sshhh," said Elisabeth.

They were led through a network of alleys, passing goats, chickens, three half-naked children propelling a wheel down the lane with a stick. They stooped and passed through a low doorway. Inside, it was dark and smoky. Belqassim motioned for them to sit on the floor, then disappeared into a back room.

"What are we doing here?" said Simon.

"Having an adventure."

A short, chubby, bearded man entered with a tray of sweets, a copper pot, and a small stack of glasses, then placed it all on the floor before them. "Mohammed," he said solemnly, offering his hand, which was as soft as putty. "You are American, yes?"

"At last," said Simon, "someone who speaks English."

"Only a little, I'm afraid. Please, some *thé à la menthe?*"

"Yes, thank you."

He poured three glasses, placing a sprig of mint in each. "*Où est Belqassim?*" asked Elisabeth.

"Attending to business," he said, cryptically. "Please, help yourself. The pastries are very good."

They both tried one. They were absurdly sweet.

"Mmmm," said Simon.

"*Ils sont divins,*" said Elisabeth.

"My wife made them," said Mohammed. "She will be very pleased. Please, take as many as you like."

An awkward silence fell. Simon took a sip of tea, staring into his glass to have something to do.

"May I show you something, something you may find quite rare and beautiful?" He rose and left the room. In no time, he returned, carrying a large carpet, dropped it to the floor and unrolled it. It was brown with gold trim and smelled of urine. "A Berber prayer rug," he said, regarding it with admiration.

Simon glanced at Elisabeth. She started to giggle.

"And I have numerous others." He presented his carpets, one after another, rolling them out across the floor with a dramatic flourish of his arms and a "*Voila!*" Soon he was out of breath, his shirt stained with sweat. He collapsed before them, his mouth open, staring expectantly at Simon.

"Very nice," said Simon. After everything the man had gone through, Simon felt obliged to buy something. "How about the small blue one."

"A fine choice," he said. "And because you are friends of Belqassim I will make a special price."

Suddenly, Belqassim appeared, as if on cue, to advise them.

Their scheming was obvious, and yet Simon was impressed by their methods, how they corralled him in so efficiently. Without argument, Simon handed over the sum Belqassim suggested. He shook Mohammed's soft hand again. Then he hefted the unwieldy carpet he would never have any use for into his arms and followed Belqassim back the way they had come.

As they passed through the *souqs* again, Simon saw a man standing against a wall, shouting at people. His hair was long and matted, his *djellaba* filthy and torn. Children played near him, running up and touching him as if dared to do so. He stomped and growled and wielded his arms. Spittle flew from his lips. He pointed to the heavens and cried out as if in pain. Now and then people placed money in the dirt before him in a reverential way.

Simon stopped and set his carpet down. "Who is that?"

Elisabeth repeated the question to Belqassim.

"*Un Mejdoub—un halluciné bienheureux, un saint fou . . .*" Belqassim continued in a solemn tone.

"What?" said Simon impatiently. "What did he say?"

"He says it's a *Mejdoub*—a holy maniac."

"A what?"

"A crazy saint. He says he only speaks words from the Koran. Makes prophesies, cures the sick, gives barren women children. Says he's good luck."

Simon watched in wonder as the Mejdoub took in great breaths of air before launching once more into his rant. Whether genuine or not, he was certainly impressive. He could never be confused with one of those dime-store derelicts in New York City. There was an intelligence about him, a mindfulness.

"Let's go see him."

"No, Simon . . . he looks dangerous."

"Suit yourself."

As he neared the Mejdoub, he was struck by the powerful scent of roses. He took out a few dirham and placed them at his feet. *Free me of my past*, he said silently. *And transform me.* He said the phrase twice more then looked up into the Mejdoub's face, surprised by how serene and clear his eyes were. At once, the Mejdoub grabbed Simon by the wrist and pulled him close. Simon fell to his knees, stunned by the man's strength, and began to tremble. The Mejdoub stroked his head, soothing him like a dog, and whispered long Arabic phrases into his ear. Then he took Simon by the chin and lifted his face, so that he couldn't turn away. As the Mejdoub stared into his eyes, Simon felt levers being thrown, one after another, felt his mind seethe like dry ice and fall perfectly still. Finally, the Mejdoub let go of Simon and thrust his hands up into the air, calling out, "*Allahu Akhbar.*" Simon got to his feet, turned and, half-stumbling, fled without looking back.

That night a sandstorm laid siege over the village. A steady mist of sand poured in through the small window, covering every surface of the room. The wind wailed like a wounded animal. Simon reclined on the gritty sheets, sipping from his last bottle of J&B. He felt strange, as if something were coming over him, dysentery or the flu. He drank more of the whiskey, hoping to kill whatever it was that was ailing him.

As he watched Elisabeth on the floor doing yoga in her underwear, the room began to spin. She tossed her legs up over her head and balanced on her shoulders, her breathing exaggerated. Her neck seemed unnaturally bent.

"Doesn't that hurt?"

"*Non, ça fait du bien!*"

He found it absurd that the moment she finished, she would light up another cigarette. She stood and began performing what she called her warrior poses—legs spread, arms reaching outward, then bending a knee and sinking to one side. She looked coiled and deadly as if she were about to thrust a sword into some invisible foe.

The next thing Simon knew it was the middle of the night. The wind continued to howl. He could hear the date palms thrashing wildly. A thin layer of sand coated his face. Sweat poured from his body. The sheets wrapped around his legs were soaking wet. He stared up at the dark ceiling. The room seemed to throb with a bug-like presence. He drifted in and out of sleep, expecting at any moment to be devoured like a small grub. Dreams and brief glimpses of what might or might not have been reality overlapped and became indistinguishable. As much as he struggled to decipher the true strain, he could never be certain. One moment he was talking to Elisabeth, the next she was his ex-wife. Belqassim appeared with the head of a goat, smoking a *kif* pipe. The ceiling was dark then light then dark again. A doctor came, prodded his belly, stuck a thermometer in his mouth. Simon opened his eyes. "I am being transformed, *Monsieur.* There is nothing you can do." Now and then, Elisabeth and Belqassim hovered over him, whispering in French. He realized at one point he had been left alone for a very long time.

In one dream, he was having drinks with his ex-wife, Helen, and his old friend and real estate partner, Marc, when suddenly he realized with a shock that they were a couple now—that Helen had left him for Marc. Of course, why hadn't he seen it before? They kissed and nuzzled one another like newlyweds. They smiled at Simon and said how they hoped that they could all be friends now. They raised their glasses in a toast. Simon excused himself, nauseated, unable to stand being in his own skin. He understood he was in their home, a magnificent home, which had been bought and paid for, it dawned on him, with his money. He had to flee at once. He ran to the first door he spotted and flung it open. Suddenly, there before him stood the Sahara—like salvation—nothing but sand and blinding light.

II.

He woke. He could now say he was definitively awake. He sat up and looked around. He felt good, though his body looked terribly gaunt. He felt different somehow, as if he weren't fully present, but floating, indifferent. On shaky legs, he made his way to the bathroom and, barely able to lift the bucket, doused himself with cold water. He had no idea how many days he had been gone. He found a pair of pants and a T-shirt but little else. He noticed all of Elisabeth's things were gone. He dressed and left the room. It was good to breathe fresh air again. It was still early in the morning, the light low, the first birds just beginning to sing. He noticed the door to the adjacent room was open a crack and recognized one of Elisabeth's bras on the floor. He nudged the door open and saw Elisabeth and Belqassim lying naked in a tangle of sheets. The room was thick with *kif* smoke and the smell of sex. He could not bring himself to wake them. They were like children. It was almost beautiful, the two of them, limbs draped over one another, breasts and penis languishing like warm fruit. He was not surprised, he decided. It would all be lumped together into his past. On the bedside table, he saw his wallet and car keys. He grabbed the keys, then, out of curiosity, looked inside his wallet. It was empty. He placed it back on the table and glanced one last time at Elisabeth, astounded by his dispassion. As he started to leave, he grabbed two bottles of water he found at the foot of the bed, then gently pulled the door shut behind him.

He drove the Peugeot to the end of the village then continued on toward the border outpost of M'Hamid. There was no road to follow, only thin camel trails, gently undulating. Finally, the car could go no further, the sand so deep the wheels only spun in place. He grabbed the water bottles and set out in the direction he assumed was south. After several hours, he began to see the dunes of Algeria. He must have crossed the border already, he thought, passing wide of M'Hamid. He continued on, weakly, relishing the emptiness, the cleansing heat, the gradual quieting of his mind. This is what he had dreamed of all along.

At one point he realized he had been climbing the same dune for hours, taking one step then losing two. By the time he reached the crest of the dune, the sun was setting. He sat down and emptied the first bottle of water. For miles, all he could see were dunes, one after another. Soon, he thought. Then he collapsed to one side and fell deeply asleep.

He woke shivering. It was dark. He got to his feet and started walking again to stay warm. By midday, he finished the second bottle of water. He touched his face tentatively, feeling his nose, lips, cheeks and ears—crinkly with scabs. Now that the water was gone, he was surprised to find he didn't have any desires. He slumped to the sand, deciding to stay put for a while. After all, where was he going? He was already there. Sometime later, a scorpion scurried up his arm, circled his neck, then crawled down his back. He closed his eyes then opened them again, thinking it was only a moment later, though now it was night. Then he rolled over onto his back and returned to his dreamless sleep.

At some point—hours or days later—Simon sat up and realized he could no longer remember who he was, not even his name. It came, surprisingly, as a relief.

He lay back in the sand, which had risen up around him to form a sunken bed. Like a child, he let the sand sift through his fingers, enjoying the sensation.

"A pocketful of dust," he said to himself, imagining what the desert would make of him. He repeated it out loud, liking the sound of it: "A pocketful of dust." He found it soothing. He began to sing it softly like a lullaby, over and over again, until he passed out.

There were voices, a nasal, rattling bark. He strained to open his eyes and lift his head. In the distance, he saw tall, gangly creatures with blue heads moving toward him. As they drew closer, he understood what he was seeing: Berber nomads, their heads wrapped in indigo turbans, riding camels. Unable to remain conscious, Simon closed his eyes and drifted off again. When he came to, he was sitting on the back of a camel in a long line of camels walking across the desert. A small sack covered with fur hung sloshing around his neck. He opened it and drank some. It tasted sweet, slightly fermented. He guzzled the entire contents and immediately threw up. Behind him, one of the blue-headed nomads laughed.

They set up camp in the evening and led him to a place near the fire. One by one the nomads came up to him and looked searchingly into his eyes. They seemed pleased by him, even excited. Simon kept hearing the word Mejdoub being passed around. He knew that word from somewhere but couldn't quite place it. Perhaps it was his name. Two of the nomads lifted him to his feet and began walking him around the fire. Everyone started singing and clapping. Simon could barely walk but soon found himself moving on his own. The wind picked up and the flames leapt high into the air. Simon could remember nothing, although his body seemed to know what to do. Instinctively, he took one of the nomads into his arms and began to perform the rudiments of a waltz, spinning around the fire, faster and faster, while the nomads cried out "*Allahu Akhbar!*" Simon realized that at any moment he might collapse, but somehow he hung onto the grinning nomad and, rearing back his head, shouted "*Allahu Akhbar*" into the night sky.

Mykonos (circa 1988)

W e left Athens in the evening, on an overnight ferry to Mykonos. The ship rumbled beneath us at a snail's pace, shuddering with such violence we imagined something must be wrong with the engine. The cabin smelled of diesel so we stayed on deck, letting the warm wind wash over us and watching the sunset bleed out over the Aegean Sea. After a while, M. returned to our stateroom, complaining of a stomachache, while I remained on deck to watch the stars. As I lay there, staring up into the night sky, I had the sensation of looking down upon a buzzing, luminous metropolis—full of traffic jams, racing freeways, city blocks and skyscrapers with every window lit. The stars wheeled, darted, scintillated above me, each distinct, detonating over and over again in perfect silence.

I felt far from everything, free to remake myself.

In our mid-twenties, we had arrived in Greece so I could work for *Rococo* (the Greek equivalent of *Armani*), who had booked me to model their suits and do their ad campaign. And, since neither of us had ever been to Greece before, we decided to stay.

M. was still awake when I returned to our stateroom—moaning and tossing in bed. She looked possessed, glassy-eyed, her long, blond hair matted and soaked with sweat.

"My God!" I said.

"Maybe it was the lamb," she whispered between gasps—having eaten lamb that evening in the ship's mess. Then, suddenly enraged, she cried out: "Why won't this fucking boat stop shaking!"

She continued to moan and hold herself for another hour, until finally she fell asleep.

I figured whatever it was would pass by morning. But the next day, as we drifted into Mykonos harbor, she was pasty and green, sweating profusely, and still in pain. I helped her to shore, bags slung over my shoulder, and chose a simple pension within walking distance of the harbor. It was clean and white with a porch overlooking the sea. I left her in bed while I hurried to the pharmacy to find something for the pain.

It was an aesthetic marvel, the island: the bleached buildings with blue shutters, the stark volcanic rock, the views of fishing boats and cerulean water. But as I searched for a pharmacy, a doctor's office, I was indifferent to it all—only thinking of M.

I passed the street market, where tourists bartered for produce, young gay men fingered jewelry and scarves, and a table of old Greek men looked on with amusement, throwing back shots of ouzo. It was only ten, but already the men were drinking, and the sun splashed violently against the whitewashed walls.

By the time I returned to the room with medicine, she looked worse. She lay writhing in bed, cramping as if in labor. "I'll get a doctor," I said.

"No," she cried, "don't leave!" She was naked except for a T-shirt, cupping her pubic bone, raging, hair wild.

From between her legs, a pinkish fluid spread across the sheets. It struck me then, with staggering force: she was having a miscarriage—the miscarriage of a child neither of us knew she was carrying. A moment later, she arched her back and groaned, and the fetus appeared. I could not connect what I was seeing—the delicate, membranous skull, eyes, fingers—to my ordinary world. How could this tiny dead child exist in the same reality as, say, the camera on the bedside table, or the book (whose bold letters signified nothing)?

M. propped herself up on her elbows and looked between her legs. She began keening softly, twisting her head from side to side. Then the wail grew in pitch until it reached a full-throated cry. I had never understood the word *hysterical* till now. "My baby!" she shrieked.

Was it a boy, girl? I didn't check, didn't want to know. I scooped it up with a wad of toilet paper and threw it in the trashcan, then covered it with more paper—wanting to erase, deny, its very existence.

"No," I lied, "no, it was only blood."

Still wailing, she looked at me with horrified eyes.

I felt embarrassed. By what—our cluelessness? That someone might hear? I felt as if we had done something terribly wrong.

I grabbed her by the shoulders. "Stop it," I said. But she kept screaming—a pure exhalation of grief, her voice swooping up and down.

I slapped her face and she fell silent, aghast, mouth ajar. "You're all right," I said, trying to get her to look at me. I hugged her; she felt limp in my arms and shuddered. Though her pain was gone, she had withdrawn to some far corner of her consciousness and stared without focus.

The next day, we took the first ship back to Athens, then a taxi directly to the hospital.

M. waited for hours, lying on a gurney in the hallway, with nothing but a hospital gown to cover her—her long tan legs exposed. The bleach rising off the floors stung my eyes and the pale green walls echoed with anxious voices. The doctor, when he finally arrived, could only speak a handful of English words—"yes," "okay," "no problem"—which he repeated at random, then abruptly walked away.

Sometime later, an orderly appeared and wheeled her down the hall. "Don't worry," I said, "everything will be okay"—which came out sounding asinine. I followed, holding her hand, until we reached a set of doors beyond which I wasn't allowed to go.

While the procedure took place, I fled the hospital to clear my mind and found a quiet side street with thick vegetation growing on either side and forming a canopy overhead. It was late-afternoon and hot—a dry desert heat that instantly dried the sweat from my skin. As I walked along the shaded street, I was plagued with conflicted feelings of regret and relief. I wasn't ready to raise a child or marry or even stay in one place. And I didn't see M. as a mother or wife (more a consumed artist). But I couldn't help but imagine what the child might have been like, the trajectory of his life. I imagined a quiet, towheaded boy, prone to bouts of giggling, with large, clever eyes. And, for a moment, I imagined the love between us—as if he truly existed in the world.

Wherever his soul was headed, I wished it well.

When she returned from the operation, she looked shell-shocked and defeated. And with an armful of flowers and a stack of German fashion magazines, I declared my love. But something had changed between us. I felt it immediately. As she lay in bed in the recovery room and the windows darkened, she spoke of spending more time in Germany with her family, of going back to school to study photography, of settling down somewhere . . . in Berlin perhaps. And I understood that our journey together was coming to an end.

As we left the hospital together that evening, she leaned heavily against me and, with slow steps, we advanced toward the taxi. It was quiet out and still warm and the tops of cypresses moved in the breeze. At once, the urge to belong flared up inside me, though I foresaw only years of wandering ahead. I looked up into the night sky, hoping to find stars, but the pollution and city lights prevented me from seeing anything.

Cathy Englis

The Mexican Messiah

And what do you remember, finally, when . . . the streets are empty of devotion and hope . . . ?

Is the memory thin and bitter and does it shame you with its fundamental untruth . . . ?

Or does the power of transcendence linger, the sense of an event that violates natural forces, something holy that throbs on the hot horizon, the vision you crave because you need a sign to stand against your doubt?

—Don DeLillo, *Underworld*

I.

Evening News

Catharine Beauregard Stein came in from the garden as if out of a furnace, the knees of her jeans coated with earth. She stood there for a moment, in the entrance of her house, dripping with sweat, savoring the first cold rush of air conditioning. It was August, early evening, a wet Virginia heat.

At seventy-two, a widow, Catharine felt more or less content to live alone. She still carried herself, she liked to think, with the dignity of a debutante, and though her hair was gray now, she artfully streaked it blond. She had a kind, noble face, gently ravaged from years of sun-worshipping, with steel-blue eyes that tended to stare off into some middle distance. She came across as dreamy, aloof.

She took off her gardening gloves and dropped them to the floor, then stepped out of her muddy sneakers. She went into the kitchen and poured herself a tall glass of iced tea, then, in her stocking feet, shuffled into the living room and collapsed onto the couch. She was exhausted and filthy, having gardened all day, too tired even to bathe. She switched on the television, as she did every day at this hour, just in time for the evening news. She enjoyed the news, as a good-for-you distraction, never seeing it as having anything to do with her. She stared at the screen contentedly, watching but not watching.

Everything about the newscast was performed in its usual, reassuring way—often she would burst out laughing at the anchor's ridiculously dramatic, stylized delivery—and yet tonight there was something different about the program. She felt implicated, as if it were expressly for her.

He began to report the story of a young Mexican man named Jesús Almirez, who had captured the imagination of hundreds of thousands of Mexicans convinced he was the Messiah. "And now," said the reporter, "from Mexico City . . ." The camera then jumped back and forth between an overhead shot, as from a helicopter, and a close-up of Almirez himself as he waded through a sea of people. They crushed toward him in a frenzy, many in tears, desperate to get near him, to touch him. They fell to their knees, stretched out on their bellies in supplication.

"Good Lord!" Catharine said, sitting upright.

Close to thirty thousand people had shown up to hear him speak at the Zocalo, the central plaza in Mexico City. As he walked through the crowd, he appeared calm, smiling and greeting people as he passed. He was thirty-two, according to the report, but looked years older, and at the same time like a child. He was small and brown, dressed in a beige threadbare cotton suit, with the faintest trace of a beard and mustache. But it was his eyes that caught her attention. They were large and bright, as if lit from within, and so familiar, though she couldn't quite place them. In the fleeting instant Jesús's glance now turned to the camera, Catharine caught her breath and felt something very subtle pass between them.

Before Catharine knew it, the segment had ended and she was watching the weather, promising yet another scorching day. Catharine turned off the television and took a deep breath, clearly shaken on some level she could not name. Perhaps the Pope could summon such devotion, she thought, but never in her life had she seen anything like this. She closed her eyes and found that she could review the image of his face in detail. She felt she would burst with emotion or become overwhelmed with sleepiness. Her childhood came rushing back: cold mornings in the convent, saying her prayers by rote, Mother Superior's ever-watchful gaze, and the miraculous morning when she slipped into perfect stillness as if God had walked into the room.

Her first impulse was to go straight upstairs, pack her bags, and catch the next flight to Mexico City. But she sat a moment longer—as the ice cracked and melted in her glass, and Zack, her black lab, scratched at the screen door—until the impulse passed and was replaced by a dozen everyday concerns. Then she got up to make herself some dinner, smiling to herself at her foolishness.

II.

Lo Siento

Donny DeCecco pulled up in front of his old house, left the pickup running. He honked twice and waited. The house could use another coat of paint, a better watering system. The grass was brown and would only get worse. He honked again.

A moment later, Maria's head peered out from behind the front door. "You're early," she called. "The kids aren't ready."

"Jesus," Donny said under his breath, shaking his head.

"Don't give me that," Maria said from the doorway. "You can come back in half an hour, like you're supposed to."

Donny revved the engine, threw it into gear, and sped off.

He drove a few miles till he reached a 7-Eleven and pulled into the parking lot. He lit a cigarette and sat a moment, wanting nothing more than to throttle his ex-wife. Even at 6 PM it was murderously hot, and the damn air-conditioning had given out months ago. He went in and bought a six-pack, then returned to his truck and downed two beers before he realized it was time to head back.

It had been six months since the divorce and Donny still felt raw. "*Lo siento*, Donny," she had said one day, "I don't love you anymore." But Donny wondered if she had ever loved him, wondered if she hadn't just seen a gringo with a good job and a nice home and a way out . . . How he had prayed for her to love him again—and wept, yes, wept—but there was no turning back a woman's heart once it had turned. He was thirty-five now and lived alone in a one-bedroom apartment near the airport, overlooking a billboard and Rancho Drive. Tall, stoop-shouldered, and balding, he often joked that he was the only Italian in Vegas not in the mafia, and he would have moved back to Queens in a heartbeat if it weren't for the kids.

He had moved to Vegas in his twenties, drawn by the construction boom, and met Maria at a church dance. Her family, three generations of Nogales women, had watched as he led her to the dance floor and performed the rudiments of a waltz, her breasts nudging up against him. She was small and voluptuous, her hair long and black. She looked no older than eighteen. And the way her hand fit into his, like a child's, made Donny feel powerful.

When he pulled up in front of his old house—now Maria's house—his mother-in-law was standing in the driveway holding Max and Rosa's hands. So, she won't even face me, he thought—sends her goddamn mother out instead . . . A rotund, toad-like Mexican woman, Maria's mother scowled at Donny as he stepped out of the truck's cab. "Hey Rosa, hey Max-Max . . ." He squatted and hugged his children, ignoring his mother-in-law. They were beautiful children— people said it all the time: brown-eyed and olive-skinned, with sandy hair. Max, at six, wore his favorite Spider-Man T-shirt, while Rosa, eight, wore a simple yellow sundress.

"Asegúrate de traer a los niños el domingo antes de las seis," said the grandmother.

Donny looked to Rosa for translation.

"Abuela says have us back before six on Sunday."

Donny grunted. He could feel the old woman's eyes on him. "Okay, Super-champs, grab your things, say goodbye."

They hugged their grandmother, then waved to their mother, who stood waving from the living room window.

It was always wrenching, the handing over of the children. And why was he the bad guy? *He* hadn't given up on the marriage; *he* hadn't betrayed the family. And yet here he was, looked on by all as the one who had deserted, and been banished, and would now take them away.

They all climbed into the truck and Donny started the engine. The children continued to wave and smile, as their mother waved back from the window and their *abuela* wad-dled up the driveway toward the house.

III.

Luminous Bare Feet

Catharine rose early after a strange, fitful sleep and made her way to the foot of the bed, where she got down stiffly onto her knees and, placing her head into the plush white carpet, bowed before the picture of Christ on the wall. It was a small painting, a tad kitschy, of Jesus standing in a white robe against a blue background with a subtle halo around his head, his right hand raised in blessing. Dawn poured in through the window as she said her prayers, warm against the side of her face. She preferred this representation of Christ in glory to him on the cross. She wanted to remember him for his gift of light, not for his suffering.

Numerous times throughout the night, she had woken from an ongoing dream, soaked in perspiration, with some important but unrecognizable name or word rising from deep inside her. It had sounded like an eastern language, Arabic or Hindi—a long string of vowels. She could recall nothing of the dream, only an afterimage—vaguely menacing stick-like figures in a scorched landscape—but she knew it had been intense. The synapses of her brain felt raw with activity.

With *amen* she lifted her head and looked up one last time at the picture of Jesus. Then an image popped into her head, another detail recalled from the dream: a pair of unadorned bare feet. They were placed side by side and seemed to carry a ritualistic significance. But to whom did they belong? As she stood up and adjusted her nightgown, a wave of dizziness passed over her and she had to steady herself against the wall before going to wash up.

SHE DROVE THROUGH horse country, past miles of rolling, verdant pastures, delineated by split-rail wooden fences, which soon gave way to subdivisions, malls, parking lots, high rises. It had been a quaint town twenty years ago, when she first moved to the area, a distant satellite of Washington, the few streets tree-lined, friendly. Now it was as if a virus had devoured the land, every day more concrete, another steel and glass façade. She pulled into the parking lot next to the Hospice Center, left the engine running, reluctant to abandon Mozart or the air-conditioning. Twice a week she volunteered at the center—not that she could offer much help. Ever since her husband's death, she had been searching for a purpose, something to pour herself into. Most of the time she felt she was in the way, but she did what she could—giving sponge baths, emptying bed pans, reading stories.

The nurse inserted a long rubber tube into the hole cut into the patient's windpipe, vacuuming up phlegm. A small silver ring edged the hole like a washer. Catharine wondered how an incision in the body could be kept from closing. Gently, she wiped Mr. Renaldo's brow with a wet washcloth. There was barely anything left of him, his form lost beneath the sheets, his skull shriveled, feathered with wisps of white hair. The nurse—Becky or Betty—was stocky, muscular in her movements, arms flexing as she shoved the tube in and drew it out as if under fierce resistance. Her concentration was such that she didn't look up or say a word. There was no escaping the slurping sound, the phlegm rattling in his chest. The hole, despite its small size, gave off a strong odor of decay. Catharine felt lightheaded and busied herself taking in the room: the light-green walls, the bronze crucifix above the bed, the sealed windows overlooking the parking lot. Mr. Renaldo's eyes were shut, moving violently beneath the lids. She wondered where the morphine had taken him as it steadily dripped into his veins. She rinsed out the washcloth, warm with his fever, and continued to stroke his forehead with it, whispering whenever he seemed to grow anxious: "It's okay, Mr. Renaldo. Everything's all right."

Then she thought of Sam, her husband, of how, nearly twenty years before, he had waved the priest away when he came to administer last rites. In a way, she admired her husband's conviction, his faith in himself before any other source of salvation—even as his eyes were fixed in that twilight stare, his body gutted with nothing left for the cancer to rage against.

The next thing she knew she was lying on the floor. Betty or Becky was waving ammonia beneath her nose. Somehow, she had ended up on the opposite side of the room, a good ten feet from where she had been standing. As she came back to consciousness, she recognized the entire right side of her body felt bruised.

"I don't have time for this foolishness—you hear me? You can't go flopping around like some big dead fish."

She must have made quite a racket going down. Half a dozen nurses stood over her. Even Mr. Renaldo strained to lift his head. Embarrassed, she tried to sit up. Hillary, another volunteer, helped her to her feet then led her to a chair in the waiting room and handed her a cup of water. "You okay, hon'?" Hillary wore a gray synthetic pantsuit that matched her short-cropped hair.

"Low blood sugar. That's all."

Hillary reached up and felt along Catharine's head, smoothing the stray hairs. "Dear, you've got quite a lump here. Maybe I should get one of the nurses."

"No, no, it's nothing." In a sudden, mad rush, the full memory of what had just occurred came to her. In the brief time she was unconscious, she had resumed the dream from last night, although it was charged in a way unlike any dream she had ever had before. At once, she had been transported into a realm that seemed more real, of far greater importance than this one. There was the same familiar desert landscape, the odd stick-like figures that vacillated on the horizon, and, in the near distance, a pair of luminous bare feet.

IV.

Fire on the Mountain

A Dire Straits song played on the radio—"Sultans of Swing"—as the kids bounced and wiggled in their seats to the music. The stoplight turned red and Donny braked behind a station wagon. On its rear bumper, the sticker read, "HONK IF YOU LOVE JESÚS," then, in smaller letters, "ALMIREZ." He'd seen the bumper sticker before and others like it. Was the driver Mexican? From behind, he couldn't tell. He waited, seething . . . What's wrong with these people, he thought—that they can so easily cast Jesus aside for this . . . this *charlatan*? Maria and her mother—hell, the whole family—had gone the same way. And he'd be damned if he'd let his kids pray to some lunatic. In a way, he even blamed Almirez for the collapse of his marriage. Up until he showed up in their lives, they still had their faith to hold them together. Every Sunday they went to Mass as a family and Donny felt sanctified, his hope restored. As he saw it, after the passion had burned out between them, the one thing he and Maria still had in common was the Church. Now even that was gone.

A moment later, the light turned green, but the station wagon remained. Donny put his hand to the horn, then stopped himself. Damn if I honk for that son of a bitch. He flashed his lights instead, and the station wagon moved forward.

Donny drove to a playground near his apartment building, deserted except for a dusty-brown mongrel that sniffed and scratched at the dirt. He sat on a bench and watched distractedly as his children climbed the jungle gym. Every few minutes a plane passed overhead, accompanied by a deafening wash of sound. Donny looked out beyond Rancho Drive to where the town ended, and the desert began. There wasn't a tree in sight and little vegetation besides a handful of saguaros. The sun, a deep orange sphere, hovered just above the horizon. Was this where he would spend his days, on land so hot and barren only snakes and cacti survived? It was a kind of purgatory, every aspect of his life a sad reminder of what he had had before. And each day the sun continued to scorch the earth around him.

When Donny returned his attention to Max and Rosa, they were standing nearby, looking bored.

"What's for dinner?" Rosa said.

"I want margherita pizza," said Max.

Donny felt a moment of anxiety as he realized two of the weekend's highlights—park and pizza—would soon be exhausted.

They returned to the truck and Donny drove to a pizza place where he bought pizza by the slice, and they sat on stools facing a brick wall while they ate. The air smelled sweet—of cooked tomatoes and cut-rate cheese. Donny kept looking at the Italian girl who rang them up, a plump girl with cleavage and Medusa-like hair. To sleep with another woman, he thought, might cure him of Maria, but he knew he didn't have the courage to say more than hello.

Rosa paused mid-bite, sat upright, and turned to Max. "We forgot to say our prayers." Max, already covered with tomato sauce, looked chastened and solemnly placed his pizza back on the plate. The two children then bowed their heads and whispered to themselves in Spanish. This was new, thought Donny, the prayer unfamiliar, no doubt linked to this Almirez business. When they lifted their heads again, they returned to their pizzas.

"What was that all about?"

The children looked at each other. "Before we eat, Mommy wants us to say our prayers." Rosa spoke as if it had been rehearsed.

"Mommy taught us," said Max, wiping his mouth on his shirtsleeve.

"I see . . ." said Donny. "And who are you praying to, Max-Max?"

Max looked confused by the question. "The man on the news . . .?"

Rosa giggled nervously. "He's not *the man on the news,* silly."

"You mean the Mexican man?"

The boy looked to his sister, as if unsure of what he was allowed to say.

"It's okay, Champ, you can tell me."

Staring down at his pizza, Max nodded cautiously.

"But, Daddy, it's all right," Rosa said. "It doesn't mean anything . . ."

The confirmation that his children prayed to some derelict, a former mental patient, who wandered the desert without a pot to piss in, struck Donny like a two-by-four to the side of the head.

"Finish up," he said. "We're leaving." He stood, knocking over the stool, which struck the floor behind him with a loud bang.

The children jumped in their seats and began eating faster, Max stuffing the folded pizza into his mouth.

There was no one to rail against, no one to recognize the injustice, the absurdity. He needed everything to wind back, make sense again. On the jukebox, a country singer sang "Fire on the mountain . . ." over and over again. Donny clenched his jaw and fists, unsure of what to do with all that was brimming inside him.

V.

The Unstruck Sound

Catharine sat at the piano, working her way through the Brandenburg Concerto. As the metronome ticked back and forth, she strained to keep up, lagging ever so slightly behind. It was late afternoon and the sun poured into the den, drawing out the oranges and reds in the Oriental rug. Upstairs, for five days now, her bags had remained packed at the foot of her bed. Each day, she was reminded of her impulse to leave yet continued to do nothing. Why—what was holding her back? A cardinal slammed against the plate glass window in front of her—a streak of red—then dropped to the ground. Catharine paused while the metronome continued its relentless clip. The bird then gathered itself and flew off again. Who was he really, Almirez? She'd heard the stories, news reports, seen the documentaries. But how to explain her feelings?

He was an orphan, she'd read somewhere, with no education to speak of, born on the edge of the now famous Bordo Poniente landfill outside Mexico City. He'd spent his early years as a beggar on the streets of the capital, before being sent to the Orcaranza Asylum, where he was diagnosed with schizophrenia, medicated, and remained until the age of sixteen. After that, there was a biographical gap of nearly ten years. Some said he wandered the desert like an ascetic; others claimed he worked at a restaurant in León. He had been jailed, more than once, she'd learned, for inciting public disturbance. He swore no allegiance to church, faith, or tradition, and spoke very little, though was famously recorded on 60 Minutes as saying: *"Todo existe dentro de mí." Everything exists within me.*

He had been appropriated (and rejected) by numerous traditions. . . . Some said he was the risen Christ; others claimed he was the reincarnation of Buddha or Krishna, the resurrected Zoroaster or Muhammad... They called him a conman, madman, magician, fraud. In parts of Latin America, he was Quetzalcoatl come again, the Aztec god of wind and rain—the great feathered serpent (in human form). And for some, he was all of these—the formless one who takes all forms.

In one story, Almirez had been passing along the tiled platform of the Balderas Metro station in Mexico City, trailed by a swarm of followers, when he paused to speak with a beggar and her deformed child. He reportedly stroked the woman's cheek and placed his hand on the misshapen head of the toddler. The next day, at the exact spot where the woman had been seated, there was now a mark on the white tile floor, a brown water stain in the approximate shape and size of a face that looked remarkably like the face of the Virgin of Guadalupe—the dark-skinned saint of Mexico and savior of the poor. People from all over the country began flocking to the subway station as if it were a pilgrimage site, calling it a miracle.

What was she to make of such stories? She'd seen the photos. And it did look like a woman's face. But was it a miracle, or simply a water stain? Part of her wanted to believe Almirez was the real thing, while another part hoped to prove he was a fake, if for no other reason than to go back to her normal existence. Because now that there was the possibility that such a being walked the earth, she could hardly bear her small, insignificant life.

She reached up and stilled the metronome as silence settled over the room. Zack, lying beneath the piano bench, groaned and twitched in his sleep. She stood, feeling a desperate need to move, marched toward the front door, and flung it open, where a wave of near-tropic heat enveloped her. She turned and said, "Come on, boy," and Zack struggled to his feet and trotted stiff-legged after her.

She walked around the house with Zack by her side, admiring her garden, occasionally stopping to pull up a weed, careful not to get dirt on her skirt. It was a big place, colonial-style, set up on a hillside, with close to twelve acres of open field and pine forest and a nice view of the Potomac. She loved the steady wash of sound in the distance. They set off together across a wide field and passed beneath a lone horse-chestnut, its massive canopy spread out above them.

For an instant, Catharine pictured Almirez as in a snapshot, his simple peasant's face, and although she couldn't say from where it came, she felt an unreasonable longing for the man.

Having found a stick, Zack bumped up against her leg with it. She took it from his mouth and tossed it down the hill. He tore after it, came back prancing, and dropped it at her feet. Catharine picked up the stick—now covered with saliva—as the dog watched, panting, coiled with anticipation. She tossed it again, then drummed on her knees, while Zack ran back with it. "That a boy. Bring it here." But this time he sank to the ground and commenced chewing on the stick, pinning it between his paws, watching her, then pretending not to. When she reached for the stick, he made a playful growl. "Aren't we ferocious," she said, then stood bolt upright, suddenly reminded of the strange guttural sound she had heard in her dream the other night. It had sounded like a foreign voice, deeper than her own, closer to vibration than language.

A stillness passed over her and she closed her eyes. Her head grew hot, and she found herself swaying. The sound was there again, emanating from all around her—the tops of the trees, the river in the distance, the grass beneath her feet. Fluttery serpentine movements rose up her spine as the sound became louder. Her breath grew long and deep and she thought she might collapse but remained standing, as if an invisible hand were supporting her from behind. She felt at once euphoric and horrified. Starting to panic now, she forced herself to open her eyes, as if tearing herself from one reality to another.

Before her, the world appeared shattered into infinite, disparate parts of color and light—each reverberating with the unstruck sound—like a puzzle in disarray. She watched in astonishment as the world pulsed and scintillated around her—not as matter but as pools of thought or feeling.

Gradually, as the sound faded, the world began to right itself again, as the various pieces rearranged themselves into a familiar light. For a few moments, she just stood there, closing and opening her eyes. The experience had been so unnerving she was no longer certain that the reality she saw wouldn't all of a sudden scramble itself again.

Zack, clearly upset, stood up and barked twice, dropping his stick.

VI.

Saguaro

The stillness of church always made Donny feel anxious—as if some violent upheaval were about to take place. Max and Rosa, sitting on either side of him in the pew, looked as restless as he felt—Max picking his nose while Rosa pulled at the lace hem of her skirt, beginning to unravel it. He had made a bargain with them the day before: he would let them watch cartoons as long as they went to Mass. But now, he could see, they were regretting that decision, which was understandable but still pissed Donny off. The bench creaked as he shifted his weight, his knees jammed up against the pew in front of him. Frankincense and the smell of old wood wafted through the great hall. Shafts of light poured down from the domed edifice, thick with swirling specks of dust.

Father Michael, seventy and gaunt, with a bulbous Irish nose, quoted from Corinthians: "Even Satan," he pronounced, "disguises himself as an angel of light." Donny wondered if this was a reference to Almirez, and if the priest felt the same way: that Almirez was a threat to their collective faith. He remembered—wasn't it just a few years ago?—the chapel filled with parishioners. Now it was nearly empty. Could this be Almirez's doing as well? He imagined the Church crumbling before his eyes, the Vatican, all the great cathedrals, reduced to dust—cardinals, priests, even the Pope, divested, aimless, like vagabonds.

Father Michael continued: "We need to nurture our faith," he said, "and remain steadfast, no matter the temptation …" He seemed tired and frail, his voice barely above a whisper. " … no matter how new and exciting and popular it may seem. Christ's sacrifice is relevant at every moment."

They approached for the Blessed Sacrament—Max, then Rosa, then Donny—and the priest placed a coin-sized wafer on each of their tongues, repeating, "The body of Christ … the body of Christ … the body of Christ …"

DONNY PARKED in front of his old house. It was quarter to six, the sun still raging and high. For once he was early. He got out of the truck and, holding Max and Rosa's hands, led them up to the house, backpacks slung over his shoulder. Their *abuela* stood in the doorway with her arms crossed. Donny didn't bother greeting her or looking her in the eye. He squatted and hugged his children, kissing each on the cheek, then handed over their bags. "See you next week," he said. "Love you, Rosa. Love you, Max-Max."

"Goodbye, Daddy," they said—the word *Daddy* hitting him with unexpected force.

Then Donny stood and, despite the great emptiness unfolding inside him, collected himself and walked back to his truck.

HE DROVE OUT beyond the city limits to a stretch of desert where people dumped unwanted things—old sofas and cars, antiquated TVs, one of those helmet-style hair dryers. He stepped out of the pickup, holding a six-pack in one hand, a pistol in the other—the Glock .45 caliber—and climbed the small ridge, where he found a large, flat rock to sit on. He took off his boots and socks, his jeans and T-shirt, and finally his underwear—enjoying the sensation on his bare skin of sun and cooling air.

Sitting bare-assed on the rock, Donny finished one beer after another as the sun bobbed on the horizon. He looked off into the distance for a target and spotted a saguaro cactus, about eight feet tall and thirty yards away, backlit by the setting sun and looking vaguely like a cross. He stood, released the safety, and aimed the Glock at the cactus. As he pulled the trigger, the pistol jumped in his hand. There was an ear-splitting report, followed by the smell of cordite, and a second later, the bullet ripped a chunk of flesh out of the saguaro. He adjusted his aim and stance and, within thirty seconds, emptied the entire cartridge into the plant. Then he went back to the truck to get more beer and ammunition.

After a while, he felt the beer's effects, wobbling slightly after each discharge, missing more often than not. The top of the cactus drooped to one side, like a head cocked, held together by a filament of flesh. He had begun to imagine the saguaro as a man standing with his arms spread and was determined to knock the head clean off. The sun was all but gone now, the sky spanning from pink to mauve to cobalt blue. He could feel the cold descending but couldn't be bothered to stop and look for his clothes.

He missed his family, he realized, not wanting to go back alone to his apartment, but hated his wife—felt the hatred as something tangible inside him—while, at the same time, still loved her. How could that be? Then he thought of Almirez—the source, as he saw it, of so much gone wrong. "Messiah, my ass," he said out loud. The man needed to be held accountable. He reloaded the Glock and fired at the cactus with renewed passion—which soon turned to frustration, then to rage. "Drop, you son-of-a-bitch!" But it wouldn't drop. As the darkness pooled around him like oil, he began to shiver, and continued to shoot, howling at the ravaged thing, trying to hold back the tears, though they came nevertheless. At last, the head detached and fell to the ground with a thud.

VII.

Hermanas

Catharine rolled down her window as hot desert wind poured into the car. The taxi drove through desolate, parched land, the sun low, hovering behind a veil of dust. She saw nothing but prickly pear and tumbleweed and now and then a saguaro. After flying all day—from Washington to Mexico City to Durango—she felt on the verge of a migraine. She closed her eyes and let her head fall back against the headrest.

With her heavy purse draped over her, she recalled the sensation of being pregnant, the fullness and weight, the nestling presence. And she remembered the shame she felt at sixteen, the shame in her parents' eyes. "How is that even possible—in a convent?" her father had demanded. She had slept with Jason, a neighborhood boy, at home one weekend . . . because, she recalled, he had long black hair, smelled of nutmeg, and said he liked her eyes. She felt pressured by everyone to give up her baby girl—the only child she would ever have—the moment she was born. And, as the nurse took her away, she knew she had made a mistake.

Catharine felt the familiar guilt rise up inside her, for which she understood there was no absolution.

The road ran straight and flat. Soon she drifted off to sleep, jostled by the occasional pothole, picturing herself and Zack strolling along the dark, glistening water of the Potomac.

Horns, lights, voices wrenched her back. The taxi stopped. They had reached the center of Durango. It was night out, though the bright yellow streetlights had turned everything jaundiced. The taxi inched forward in traffic, passing La Plaza de Armas—as lush and green as an oasis—where families strolled or sat on benches around a fountain. Dogs and children raced back and forth. Trumpets blared from the bandstand. And La Catedral Basilica, with its brightly lit towers, loomed over everything.

She spotted a group of Europeans or North Americans walking along the crowded sidewalk eating ice cream—no doubt there for Almirez. Then she noticed the posters on every wall, each poster the same: a crude drawing of Almirez smiling, with his arms spread wide. The caption read, *Un Santo Camina Entre Nosotros.*

The commercialism disgusted Catharine and she wondered if she had made a mistake by coming. She felt lucky to have found a room—after all, the world seemed to have descended upon Durango—but she was still unsure why she was there.

Would she even recognize whether or not Almirez was the real thing? What if she had come face to face with Christ himself? she thought. Would she have been able to recognize *his* divinity? It was a point of self-reckoning—for how many, she wondered, had failed to see Christ for who he was?

She felt drawn, as if by an invisible force, and felt something close to love. Though how was that even possible? She only knew the man through news reports, and many of those were contradictory. Maybe he was nothing more than a myth, a child's fantasy, built upon hope and the promise of salvation.

She had overheard two Americans on the flight from Mexico City: There were more alleged miracles . . . Almirez had apparently cured an old man of deafness by blowing in his ears, cured an old woman of Alzheimer's by crying out, *"¡Se ha ido!"* and tapping her forcefully on the head. But were these rumors, parlor tricks, the result of a calculated dissemination? She shook her head. It was almost comical.

Her headache had returned, rising from the back of her neck, and descending from her temples. When the two separate pains met, she was sure her head would explode.

The taxi swung right, down a narrow unlit alley, made two more turns then stopped at a dead end. The driver turned, his mustache and sideburns salt-and-pepper-colored and unkempt. "*Este es el lugar,*" he said, pointing at a sad-looking two-story adobe building with no windows.

Catharine felt reluctant to leave the car. "*Espere por favor,*" she said, drawing from what little Spanish she remembered from high school. She got out and approached the building and knocked. A moment later the door opened. A tall, regal-looking woman in a white peasant dress appeared, her hair tied up in a bun. "*Bienvenido,*" she said. The woman helped Catharine with her bags, waited as she paid the driver, then guided her into the building. They passed through a courtyard where there was a fountain, palm trees in large clay pots and, above, a square of purple-black sky strewn with stars.

"*¿Norteamericana?*"

"*Sí,*" said Catharine.

The proprietor led her to the second floor, to a room with two small cots and a window the size of a shoebox. The room was empty except for a young woman who sat weeping.

"We are all like sisters here," said the proprietor, "with the one father . . ."

The young woman looked up, wiping away tears with both hands. Her hair was crimson, and she wore a silver ring in her nose. She sniffed and extended her hand. "Brigitte, from Germany."

"Hello Brigitte. Catharine, from America." She squeezed her hand.

"No noise, no drugs, no cooking, no smoking, no men," said the proprietor. "*Buenas noches, hermanas.*"

Once she had gone, Catharine sat down on the cot facing Brigitte. Her headache loomed suddenly. It seemed to draw force from the dryness. The girl appeared miserable. But wasn't a saint supposed to impart bliss?

"Are you all right, dear?"

"It makes no sense," said Brigitte. "All day I do nothing but cry—for no reason." She shrugged. "There's a French woman here who does nothing but laugh. Perhaps we could trade . . ." She smiled for an instant before another wave of tears swept over her.

"And when did this all begin?"

She shuddered, struggling to catch her breath. "Eight days ago . . . when I first saw him."

"Can you tell me what it's like—seeing him? I mean, is he authentic?"

"*Authentisch?*"

"Yes, tell me, please . . ." Catharine could no longer contain herself and her piercing head only added to the fervor. "Is he really the Messiah?"

Brigitte shrugged, wiped her eyes. "I don't know about any of that—what he is, what you call him. All I know is, I saw him and became like this . . ." She blew her nose. "How I end up, I don't know."

THAT NIGHT, DESPITE Brigitte's intermittent sobbing, Catharine fell into a deep sleep and, at dawn, woke breathless from a vivid dream. As she lay in the half-light, staring up at the adobe ceiling, she recalled its details . . . A line of crosses stood out against the sky. Bodies lay bundled and sleeping amongst the sand and stones. And there she observed a pair of bare feet—hers?—stepping gingerly between the sleeping forms. The rest of the dream was lost to her—except for the end: a loud bang and the sensation of water rising up to meet her.

VIII.

Rango

As the sun scorched the top of his head, Donny could feel the eyes of the foreman on him. He wanted a beer—and a woman, if he came right down to it—though neither was likely or available. On padded knees, he smoothed the surface of the foundation with a hand float, going over and over the concrete until it looked even. His knees and back ached and a steady stream of sweat dripped from his brow.

"DeCecco," the foreman called. Donny sat up and turned, relieved to change positions. "Phone for you: your *conchita.*" He grinned. "Sorry—ex-*conchita.*" Bearded, bald, with love handles spilling over his belt, the foreman sauntered back to his air-conditioned trailer—having done next to nothing all day.

Standing in the cool trailer with the phone to his ear, Donny felt goose bumps rise on his skin.

"Donny," she began in her Nogales accent—the vowels drawn out, nasal-inflected—which had first enchanted him and now only incited anger. "Next week, the children and I will visit Ramiro, Clarissa, and the little ones."

"Wait a minute—you driving? What about the weekend?"

"We'll be back Sunday."

"But that's *my* weekend."

"Take the next two, if you like. The children need to see the cousins, no?"

"No. . . . I mean, we had plans."

"What—so you can see *Superman?*" Maria laughed. "*Dios mio* . . . I'm sure it will still be there when we get back."

He closed his eyes, tightening his grip around the phone as if it were her neck, speechless. He hated it when his children went to Mexico. It stirred up fears of losing them—to their mother's land, certainly, but also to that strain that ran in their veins governed by superstition. He opened his eyes. The foreman sat staring at him, grinning.

"Donny? You there? *¿Estamos bien?*"

"Hmmm."

"*Bueno.*" And then the line went silent.

HE FINISHED HIS SHIFT and drove home squinting into the light. As he pulled up in front of his building, the sun was hovering over the airport, its effulgence streaming forth from behind the control tower like a malevolent spirit.

He turned on the air-conditioning the moment he stepped into the apartment. The room was stifling and permeated with the stench of roach spray and cigarettes. He opened the blinds as a tractor trailer downshifted below—WONDER BREAD in big red letters floating past. He grabbed a beer from the fridge and sat down at the Formica table, where he found a half-eaten banana, an empty bottle of rum, and a full ashtray. For months he had been trying to quit smoking, but inevitably there came that moment when he could not stand being in his own skin, and nothing else, short of sex, would suffice. He finished his beer, lit a cigarette, and contemplated what he would do without seeing his children for two weeks.

Donny made a scrambled egg sandwich and ate it standing up, then turned on the television and caught the tail end of the news—more on the meltdown at Three Mile Island.

He would have to see his children before they left, he thought. No, he would have to see his children now, he decided, if only for an instant—just a hug before bed. He rinsed out the pan and put on a clean shirt, suddenly inspired. Maria would raise hell, but hadn't he the right to kiss his own goddamn children goodnight?

It was dark out. In the distance, runway lights lit up a corner of the horizon. As he accelerated down Rancho Drive, passing through one intersection after another, traffic lights kept turning green for him, as if he were in a rare moment of grace.

He parked in front of his old house, light coursing from every window, and crept up to the bay window to peer inside. He could see Maria's mother and the children sprawled on the couch, the glow of the TV playing over the room, while Maria most likely tidied up back in the kitchen. If anything, the loneliness was worse now, as he looked in on his old life from the outside, like a voyeur, forever cut off from what he had created. And he knew, just knew, that he would end up alone—one of those guys that no one recognizes has died until the neighbors smell something. The scene looked so serene he couldn't bring himself to disrupt it. If he knocked now or rang the bell, the moment would be shattered—the children fired up, Maria and her mother fuming.

Resigned to his exile, Donny turned, walked back to his truck, and drove away.

The morning they were due to leave, Donny showed up in front of his old house unexpected. A taxi waited at the curb with the trunk propped open and exhaust pouring from the tail pipe. As Donny walked up the driveway in the dim light, Max burst out of the house—"Daddy! Are you going with us?"—the screen door swinging wide then slamming shut behind him.

"No, Super-champ, I just came to say goodbye."

"Oh."

Donny swept him up in his arms and planted a raspberry in the crook of his neck. The boy giggled and squirmed in his embrace. Then Donny set him down again. "So, you're taking a plane, huh?"

The boy nodded, brimming with eagerness. "Uh huh."

"Happy to see your cousins?"

A wave of confusion passed over his face.

"What is it, Bubs?"

"Nothing."

"*Nothing!*" Donny tickled him under the arms until he succumbed to laughter. "What sort of *nothing* did you have in mind, Mister Max-Max?"

His son grew pensive then. He could see him considering the question with great seriousness.

"Aren't you going to Nogales?"

"Rango," the boy said.

"Rango?"

At that moment, the screen door flew open again and Maria appeared, lugging bags out of the house. Moved by a moment of spite, Donny considered not helping, then thought better of it and took the bags from her hands.

"Oh!" she said, surprised—without the least thanks, he noted. "*¿Por qué estás aquí?*"

With Max and Maria following behind, Donny carried the bags out to the cab, stowed them in the trunk, and slammed it shut. He could make out the first sputtering of dawn as blood-orange light began to seep across the sky.

A moment later, Rosa emerged from the house, wearing her Hello Kitty backpack, followed by her *abuela*. Still half-asleep, Rosa accepted Donny's hug and kiss and whispered "Hi, Daddy" in his ear.

One by one, they climbed into the taxi, first Max then Rosa and then their *abuela*. As Maria was about to get into the car, Donny took her by the arm. "Where are you taking them?"

"We're going to be late. Let go of my arm."

"You're not going to Nogales, are you?"

"This is not the time. It's already been arranged."

"Where is Rango?"

"*¡Qué!* What are you talking about?"

"Max mentioned it. . . . What's in Rango?"

"Durango—not Rango. *¡Dios mío, eres un pendejo!*"

"You said you were going to visit the cousins . . ."

"*Sí* . . . We'll talk when we get back. Now let go of my arm."

In one deft movement, Maria shrugged out of his grasp, ducked into the cab, and closed the door. As the taxi pulled away, Donny stared after it, breathing hard.

IX.

Livestock

Before dawn, Catharine crept from her room and entered the dark streets, where people appeared out of doorways and converged, making their way to where the sky billowed with smoke. There, on the outskirts of town, a massive dump smoldered, dogs snuffling through trash. It smelled of burnt rubber and rotten meat, and a chemical taste lingered at the back of her throat. Was this some sort of rite of passage, a teaching perhaps, meant to put into perspective her life of luxury? She spotted a half-dozen children standing knee-deep in trash, sifting through the city's remains. Hadn't Almirez survived the same way as a child? She joined the long line of followers inching forward, stretching to the far hillside and beyond.

They were Mexicans mostly, a handful of gringos like herself. Catharine hunched against the cold wind blowing off the desert and followed an old goitered woman padding ahead. A chorus of dogs barked, then silence. Behind her, a young man in cowboy boots and a Stetson smiled. She smiled back. They moved single file down into an arroyo then up the other side. When she reached the crest, sunlight began spilling over the horizon. She could make out a village of tents in the distance where a crowd had gathered, a pair of TV news vans with satellite dishes on the roofs. Up and down the queue, vendors hawked peanuts and soft drinks, Almirez photos and figurines. Men gripping rifles marched the length of the line, scrutinizing every face—but for what? Her back ached, but in terms of sacrifice it was the least she could bear. She took a step forward, stopped, took another, consumed by the thought of coming face to face with Almirez.

She couldn't get over his evolution in recent weeks, from near silent to outspoken, even political. Was he setting the stage for a revolution—a reformation perhaps? She had been swept up, she had to admit, in the press's ever-escalating frenzy. There had been attempts on his life: a makeshift bomb had been discovered in a pastry box; a gunman had fired from a moving car, missing Almirez but wounding one of his followers. He had enemies . . . An Imam from Algeria had called him a defamer of Islam for saying that he and Mohammed were one and the same. The drug cartels were upset because he had called them *el azote*—the scourge— and instructed his followers to rise up against them. Even the Catholic Church was outraged, now that untold numbers across South and Central America had abandoned the Church to follow him. And then, of course, there was the United States, which took issue with his declaration that borders were *imaginario*.

As the sun began its slow arc, the air grew hot and thick. They walked along the narrow dirt path that followed the ridge. A river glistened below, a thin ribbon of light. She thought of the German girl—Brigitte?—who couldn't stop weeping. Would she, Catharine, dissolve into a similar cathartic state? Brigitte's age was wrong—decades younger than her own daughter—but she still felt a motherly solic- itousness toward the girl. She tried to imagine what her daughter might look like now, the child she gave away. Perhaps she had even passed her on the street—a business- woman in a pantsuit and heels, a housewife in sweats with children in tow, an artist in an elegant blouse with paint stains on her fingers.

Catharine felt lightheaded. There was no escaping the heat. She missed the shade of her prized horse-chestnut back in Virginia. Her sandals, she realized, were not serious walking shoes, the straps rubbing against her anklebones. They marched on. She could see a large adobe structure in the distance, surrounded by a tall, barbed wire fence. The line ahead wound its way to an opening in the fence, where guards stopped and screened each person who entered. Those around her began to whisper excitedly in Spanish. The old goitered woman turned and smiled. "*Ya llegamos,*" she said. Catharine nodded. The guards and barbed wire, the checkpoint and guns—all of it struck her as sinister. She had half a mind to turn and run.

Catharine heard a voice from behind calling her name and turned to see Brigitte racing toward her. "Catharine, wait . . ." Her eyes were red, her hair disheveled. She wore a white linen blouse whose buttons, Catharine noted, were out of sequence, and Catharine had the sudden desire to rebutton them for her. "I didn't hear you leave . . ." She turned to the man in the Stetson—"Do you mind?"—and slipped in line beside Catharine. Brigitte suddenly took Catharine in her arms with such fervor Catharine was at a loss as to how to respond. "I'm glad I found you. You know, I think I'm better today. See?" She pointed to her face, which, for the moment, had not dissolved into a spasm of tears. "I think you help me."

Catharine smiled but felt unable to speak.

"Don't be nervous," she said, "I'll be with you," and took Catharine's hand. Together they moved forward.

At last, they reached the fence, where a guard wearing sunglasses and a New York Yankees baseball cap searched Catharine's bag. Once they passed through the checkpoint, they were ushered beyond the farmhouse to a tent where hundreds of people sat cross-legged on a dirt floor. It looked like a pen for livestock and smelled faintly of manure. They waited a long time. People barely spoke and then only in a whisper. A generator rumbled nearby. A guard appeared, his rifle slung over his shoulder. "*Recién llegados,*" he said. And when no one reacted, he cried, "*¡Vamos!*"

Brigitte nudged Catharine. "That's you!"

Catharine struggled to her feet and joined a group who followed the guard into the adobe building. They passed through an anteroom and into a hall with high ceilings. The room was cool and dark, a welcome reprieve. People waited in rows. Some had food and drink. A young woman cradling an infant offered Catharine a tortilla. She thanked her and ate the tortilla slowly, which was still warm and chewy and tasted of burnt peanut oil. A group near the back sang in Spanish. Catharine slumped to the cool stone floor and closed her eyes, lulled by the repeated refrain, which circled around and around in her mind without making any sense.

X.

Somewhere South of Tucson

At 6:45 AM, Donny picked up the kitchen phone and called the foreman. "It's Donny . . ." he said. "I think I have the flu."

"Like hell you do."

"Listen, I need to take some time off." Donny threw in a coughing fit for good measure. "I've got fever, chills—the runs, for Christ's sake. Been vomiting all night . . ."

"Get your ass over here."

"I'm serious. Want me to infect everyone?"

"You looked fine yesterday."

"How 'bout this . . . I come in, throw up all over your goddamn desk, and let you decide for yourself."

"That's fuckin' disgusting." Donny could hear him breathing, sense him beginning to give in. "All right . . . whatever. Take a few days off."

DONNY SPENT THE DAY loading the truck with supplies: a cooler full of food for a week, a case of beer, eight jugs of water, a sleeping bag, a carton of Camels, his revolver and ammunition. He stopped at the bank and took out enough cash for gas, extra beer, a bribe if necessary—whatever might present itself.

It didn't take him long to figure out why his family went to Durango; Almirez's whereabouts were constantly in the news. He saw the journey as a test, a call to duty. No longer would he be a victim succumbing to life's injustices. He would save his kids, maybe even his ex-wife, confront that charlatan once and for all. He'd prove to his wife he was strong again, still worthy of her love. And he would do it for the Church—hell, for Christ himself. Someone needed to act in His name.

HE SET OUT AT DUSK, the windows open wide, and drove all night. Somewhere south of Tucson, he pulled over on a lonely stretch of desert and walked through thick mesquite to the top of a rise. He could see his truck below and the highway stretching on beyond the horizon, which still glowed with city lights from Tucson. Above him, a meteor shower was underway, thousands of stars streaming past. He lit a cigarette and watched in awe, having never seen such a spectacle, and wondered if it were a sign. But for what? Then he remembered he was on a mission, as if ordained, to vanquish the unjust. And he took it as confirmation that he was on the right track.

He returned to his truck, switched on a mariachi station full blast to stay awake, and continued to drive through the night, tires humming over the asphalt.

A FEW HOURS BEFORE DAWN, he reached the Mexican border in El Paso and presented his passport. After hours of darkness, he had to shield his eyes against the blinding lights of border control. He had hidden his gun behind the spare in back, though, to his relief, the agents didn't bother to search. Perhaps, he thought, it was the hour that allowed him to pass unchecked, or maybe it was another sign. He still had 600 miles to go. He would sleep by day, he decided, then travel in the cool of night.

By morning, the landscape was unchanged—flat, scorched earth, covered with tumbleweed, prickly pear and cacti, the odd manifestation of red, striated rock. He pulled off onto a rutted lane and parked in the shade of a boulder, laid out his sleeping bag and collapsed. In no time, he was asleep.

HIS DREAM HAD THE desperate quality of fever dreams. The world seemed dark and menacing and there was something he absolutely had to do, or all would be lost. And yet, racked with dread, he couldn't recall what it was he was supposed to do.

When he woke, it was to the sound of an eighteen-wheeler screaming past.

XI.

Zack

The room came alive with laughter. Catharine opened her eyes and there was Jesús Almirez, sitting before them on a wooden stool, his feet bare, planted to the stone floor. She stared at his feet. They were small and brown and thickly callused. Were these the feet from her dreams? He was telling jokes—or at least she assumed he was telling jokes, because everyone continued to laugh. Then, before she knew it, she found herself laughing as well, though she couldn't understand a word.

He wore his familiar beige cotton suit, tattered at the hems and sleeves. His hair—thick and black and longer than she remembered—spilled over his forehead. And he sported the same perpetually half-grown mustache and beard.

He was more playful than she expected, calling out to people, teasing, a certain deviousness in his eyes. One young woman, put on the spot, giggled, unable to speak, and hid her face in her hands. He moved through the crowd, touching people on the shoulders, or shaking their hands. Some bowed, or put their hands together in prayer, or made the sign of the cross. One young woman began hiccupping violently. Another wept. Almirez paused midway down Catharine's row, just ten feet away, to speak with a young man with a shaved head, who looked like he belonged in a gang. His arms were enormous and covered with tattoos. On his bicep, she discerned a naked woman riding a motorcycle trailing a wake of flames.

As Almirez approached, blood rushed to Catharine's face, and she fell into a panic. What would he want? What should she say? He leaned over her and took her hand and she was struck by his musky body odor. Had she expected him to smell like roses? His hand was cool and dry and rough, like holding a dog's paw. He looked briefly in her eyes and smiled, crow's feet fanning out in all directions. His eyes were striking, dark brown and lustrous, with specks of gold. But where was that feeling she had had before—the feeling of transcendence? Where was the proof?

"*¿Cómo estás?*" he said.

She could not summon a word, only stare dumbfounded. She had expected something profound, words to live by. Instead, she had received . . . a cliché? Just as he was about to turn away, he said one last thing, which she couldn't quite make out. But there, amongst the words, Catharine swore she heard what sounded like "Zack."

Zack? Was he inquiring about her dog—his spiritual well-being? And how in the world had he known the name in the first place? Had he read her mind, siphoned through the recesses of her life? But then, after a few minutes, Catharine began to wonder if he had actually said "*Saca,*" or maybe "*Sacro.*"

Near the end, once Almirez had left the hall, a stout, officious-looking woman in a dark suit entered, carrying a cardboard donation box labeled "AGUACATE," which she passed around from row to row.

XII.

A Cloud of Dust

At dawn, on the outskirts of Durango, Donny pulled over to pee. He parked next to a grove of agave with spikes as tall as a house and stepped out of his truck. He felt exhausted after the long night, like some roadkill he'd passed. A few hundred yards away, he spotted the beginnings of a concrete shantytown, painted in bright pastels and extending over the desert as far as he could see. Nothing moved or made a sound, except the occasional rooster crowing. As Donny studied the pattern his urine made in the sand, he was suddenly alert to the roar of engines closing in. He turned to see a procession of jet-black vans racing past, three in all, each vehicle exactly the same, glistening in the early morning light. The license plates were blacked out and shadowy figures loomed behind tinted glass. Who were they? Donny wondered. Military? Government officials? The cartel? Only one thing was certain: they were bound headlong for Durango. And a second later they were gone, trailing a cloud of dust.

XIII.

Kondenstreifen

A warm desert wind blew through the courtyard as Catharine and Brigitte, sitting by the fountain, shared a carafe of red wine. Above them, the rooftops formed a luminous square, through which they could watch the evening sky as it gradually turned from saffron to crimson to deep blue. They spoke eagerly about their encounters with Almirez—Brigitte all but certain that Almirez had said "Zack" to Catharine, while Catharine remained unconvinced—until an easy quiet settled between them, as between old friends willing to have separate thoughts.

Catharine considered what Almirez actually believed and where it coincided with her own beliefs. His ideology seemed more Eastern Mysticism than the Catholic Church: a confluence of non-duality, reincarnation, and the promise of enlightenment. No Heaven or Hell or Church or sin or Father, Son and Holy Ghost. There was even a mantra to repeat: *No existe nada que no sea divino.* Nothing exists that is not divine—a sentiment she could not abide by. After all, would that mean that mass murderers were divine? What about a rock or a telephone? And would that make her a goddess of sorts (if only she believed)? And if everything was divine, wouldn't it then follow that everything was per-fect—despite the horror and chaos and suffering?

But that seemed to be the point, according to Almirez: everything was exactly as it should be—the design of an all-pervasive conscious force. The physical world, the world of the senses, Catharine understood, was not the final reality, but a moral battleground—a school in effect—and the entire experience a preparation of the soul, forcing every last being to evolve lifetime after lifetime.

Catharine felt too steeped in her own beliefs, she real-ized, to accept any of it. But could she legitimately follow Almirez while still disagreeing with everything he held true? And how to explain this undeniable pull she felt—which she could only define as a kind of rapture? How astonish-ing, she considered, if the emissary of the Second Coming wasn't even Christian . . . She was as mystified as before she arrived. Seeing Almirez had done nothing to resolve her state of mind.

CATHARINE LOOKED UP to find Brigitte weeping. There was no sound—just a steady stream of tears.

"Dear, what is it? There must be something …"

Brigitte shrugged and smiled as the tears continued. "Nothing I'm aware of. The usual sorrows, I suppose—like everyone …"

Catharine took a sip of wine, savoring its tartness, and waited for Brigitte to go on. The fountain sputtered beside her like a living thing.

"I had a dream last night. You and I were in a car driving through the desert—I don't know who was driving—but Almirez was with us, and he told us to go very fast. There was dust everywhere, a big cloud of it. And we couldn't see where we were going. Then suddenly we stopped. And as the dust settled, a face appeared in the window. A bearded face … and I cried out because I recognized it was my husband …"

"And then?"

Brigitte wiped her eyes. "I don't remember anything else, but I remember I was afraid."

"Oh, I've had so many strange dreams lately as well," Catharine said, "dreams that feel so real I begin to wonder if they really happened."

"Almirez says there's no difference … between the dream world and the world when we're awake. He says neither are real because both are creations of the mind."

"Good Lord—then what *is* real?"

"*Ich weiß es nicht.* Whatever there is beyond the mind …?" She said it as a question, looking as perplexed as Catharine felt.

"Tell me about your husband—I had no idea …"

"Ex," Brigitte corrected. "I try to forget …" She looked up into the night sky, her tears all but subsided. "I was young when we married. Manni much older—a drinker. He could go off like a hand grenade, without warning . . . Broke my nose once, my head, I don't remember how many ribs... We were married nine years. Can you believe that?" She shook her head in disbelief. "Then one day—a perfect spring day—I was watching a plane fly across the horizon." She swept her hand across the space in front of her. "It made this long . . . I don't know the word . . . *Kondenstreifen* we say in German."

"Vapor trail."

"Yes, vapor trail. And all of a sudden—I can't explain it—I felt this overwhelming desire to kill myself."

Catharine reached across the table to console her and touched her hand.

"The next day, I emptied our bank account and walked away—left everything. That was three months ago. And I haven't been back since . . ."

"And then you made your way here?"

"Yes. But I don't know why . . . I mean, I don't believe in God or religion. It's not like I expect anything . . ."

Catharine considered for a moment if *she* expected something. And then she realized she did. Back in the convent, they would have said Brigitte's attitude was more deserving. And she knew, of course, she was being naïve, even absurd. But, yes, deep down, if Almirez were the real thing, she expected no less than the miraculous—salvation and bliss and to penetrate the mysteries.

XIV.

The Lucky Ones

Donny drove to the center of Durango and inched his way around La Plaza de Armas in search of parking. After twenty minutes in traffic, he turned down a shaded side street and found himself lost in a maze of one-way alleys, each so narrow he could barely steer his truck through. He wasn't entirely sure what he was going to do. He only knew he needed to find his ex-wife and children and confront Almirez. By the time he circled back to La Plaza de Armas, he felt overwhelmed by the torrents of people and beat-up jalopies and mule-drawn carts, the motorcycles and buses and diesel-spewing trucks . . . and longed to return to the stillness of the desert.

He spotted an elderly couple, clearly American, in sun hats and sensible walking shoes, studying a map in front of La Catedral Basilica. Donny pulled over and leaned out of his truck window. "Excuse me . . . Hi—can you help me? I don't know if you're familiar with him or not . . . but do you happen to know where I can find Jesús Almirez?"

They approached his truck with broad smiles as if they had been waiting for him all afternoon. "Yes, of course," said the woman, bobbing her head. They spread their map out before him and pointed out the location of Almirez's farmhouse northeast of town, and the river farther north, where Almirez could be found taking his early morning walk.

Donny thanked them.

"Where you from?" the man asked.

"Vegas."

"Long way."

Donny nodded as exhaust billowed around them from a passing truck.

"We came down from Houston a few days ago. Damnedest thing . . . We used to be Baptists. Can you believe it?" He laughed, shaking his head. "Not sure what you'd call us now."

Idiots, thought Donny. He needed to get away—out of the heat and blinding light.

"I guess you could say we're the lucky ones, right?" They had that delirious, self-satisfied expression of the saved. The woman continued to nod like a madwoman.

Donny weighed his words: "Well, that's what I'm here to find out."

"Ah, so you don't know yet, do you?" the man said, hitching his trousers.

The woman came forward and placed her hand on Donny's arm. "You can doubt all you want, dear," she said, "but in the end you'll surrender . . . You'll see."

At once repelled, Donny drew away as if struck. "Well, um, I have to be going . . ." he said, putting his truck in gear. Without another word, he checked his rearview mirror and reentered the streaming traffic.

XV.

An Unanswerable Question

Catharine stood along the river in twilight, with dawn still an hour away. She could hear the water sluicing past but couldn't see it beyond the veil of mist. She marveled at so many people assembled around her—two to three hundred—bundled and shivering, waiting for Almirez to arrive. They whispered when they spoke, in reverence of the occasion. Like a child, Brigitte pressed up against her for relief from the cold. The bank rose sharply above them, boulders stacked one upon another, forcing them to gather along the rutted path at the water's edge. On the opposite side of the river, she spotted a vast plain, where dozens of cars and trucks filed into rows, headlights streaming, sending up great clouds of dust.

An infant began to fuss, and the fussing grew till only the sound of wailing filled the air. A man beside her lit up a cigarette, which smelled of stale tobacco and instantly made her feel nauseous. A separate group had gathered on the other side of the river; no one seemed to know from where Almirez would appear. The river looked shallow enough at one point to cross without getting wet and a scattering of people moved between the two sides. In small increments, a coral glow began to build on the horizon as a wave of excitement coursed through the crowd. Brigitte squeezed her hand. "Any minute now." Catharine could see those around her in more detail now—so many ages and classes and backgrounds represented. Some carried bedrolls or wore earth-toned serapes. One, in a gray three-piece suit, looked like a banker having stopped on his way to work.

"There he is," said Brigitte, pointing, and though Catharine could not see him, she could make out, in the distance, the crowds parting to let him through. Cheers erupted like those for a pop star. A few moments later, Almirez materialized before her, marching by with long strides, smiling and gesturing, expounding in a hearty voice. As soon as he went past, everyone followed, filing into place as if part of an extended conga line.

Almirez stepped off the path onto the stones of the riverbed, leading the procession across the river. Catharine shivered as the water ran cold over her sandaled feet. By the time she reached the other side, Almirez had stopped, and a great throng gathered around him. Like the aftermath of an explosion, sunlight then burst across the horizon, sweeping over the desert, suddenly warm against Catharine's face. Brigitte grabbed her by the hand and pulled her through the crowd until they were nearly standing next to Almirez in the dusty parking lot. With arms spread wide and a beatific expression, he faced the eastern sky, now ablaze with tangerine light, and recited what sounded like a prayer. Some in the group joined in. Others genuflected or dropped to their knees. Catharine found herself balking at such devotion and wondered if she had been swept up in some misguided sect.

Just then, a tall Mexican man in sunglasses and a black suit stepped forward. It took Catharine a moment before she realized he was holding a gun. "*El patrón dice, ¡Basta de tu puta mierda!*" the man said, then fired three shots at Almirez—*pop, pop, pop*—which Catharine felt resonate in her abdomen. For an instant there was silence while Almirez stood motionless, looking around at his followers as if search-ing for an answer to some unanswerable question. Then, with hands reaching out, he careened off the side of a truck and collapsed in the sand.

XVI.

Fine Glittering Particles

An hour before sunrise, Donny turned off the paved road onto the narrow dirt lane that followed the river. His head-lights swept over low desert scrub, cacti, and eerie formations of sandstone, until he came upon a wide, flat area, where dozens of vehicles gathered in rows beside the river. He chose a space close to the water, stepped out of the cab and stretched, satisfied to have found the right place, where he would finally confront Almirez. He went to the rear of his truck, to where the spare was mounted to the tailgate, and reached behind the tire. There he found the revolver, which he had fixed in place and camouflaged with black electrical tape and tore it from its housing. He stood there a moment and admired the Glock, making sure it was loaded, then slipped it beneath his shirtfront into the waistband of his jeans.

In the hope of shoring up some resolve, Donny tried to remember the quote he had found in the Old Testament back in December. He had been sitting at the kitchen table, well into a bottle of rum, when he stumbled upon the line in Deuteronomy, which struck him like a burst of white-hot light: "A false prophet," it began, "who presumes to speak in my name . . ."—something, something—"must be put to death." And though he realized carrying out such a thing would violate everything he knew to be Christian—including the Sixth Commandment—he felt reassured that, at least in this exceptional circumstance, he would still be following God's will. *For the greater good*—wasn't that the rationale, to save those who would otherwise be taken in by this heretic-fraud? But that, he knew, wasn't his true motivation. His searing sense of outrage—the need to annihilate—went far beyond any logic. For the truth was, he blamed Almirez for robbing him of his wife, his family, the inviolability of the Church, and a world that made any sense.

Donny lit up a cigarette and waited by his truck, as a glow steadily built on the horizon, watching Almirez's followers milling about in anticipation. Suddenly a cheer rose up from the opposite side of the river, accompanied by a great swirl of activity. The teeming parade moved downstream, then turned and crossed the river, coming straight at him. His stomach churned with anxiety for what he was about to do.

The sheer providence of it was staggering: Before he knew it, Almirez was standing in the parking lot directly in front of him, surrounded by a horde of what Donny thought of as his sycophants. He was smaller than he imagined and so full of energy that Donny instantly wanted to extinguish it. Almirez turned to face the sunrise, now a burnished orange, and began to deliver what sounded like a sermon. With his heart thumping wildly, Donny reached under his shirtfront and grabbed his pistol.

In that moment, he spotted his ex-wife and children. They were standing together in the crowd, holding hands, staring at Donny. He blinked twice, then three times to make sure, as his heart restarted. While Maria and Rosa looked dumbfounded, Max lifted his hand and waved.

Chastened, Donny discreetly let go of the gun, drew his hand out from under his shirt, and gave Max a tentative wave in return. *Now what?* he thought.

An instant later, there was the sound of gunfire, followed by a riot of voices. Almirez had been shot. *Almirez shot?* It didn't make sense. He had visualized the moment so many times. Had he suffered some lapse, fired in a trance? But, no, his gun was still there, cool against his waist.

Almirez reeled for a moment in place like a drunkard, stumbled against Donny's truck, then crumpled at his feet, blood already pooling around him in the sand. Instinctively, Donny rushed to his side, sank to his knees, and cradled the man's head. Almirez stared up at him, repeating breathlessly, "*Llévame a Bordo Poniente . . . llévame a Bordo Poniente . . .*" which Donny could not make any sense of.

At once, a shadow fell over Donny. He looked up to find a tall Mexican man in sunglasses and a black suit standing over him, holding a gun. The man nudged Almirez's torso with the toe of his boot, causing Almirez to moan. Seeing that Almirez was still alive, the man then raised his pistol to fire. But, in that instant, a scrum of people charged the shooter, knocking his gun away, and tackled him to the ground. Out of the corner of his eye, Donny could make out other men with guns closing in, shouldering their way through the crowd. In a fit of impulsiveness and feeling his family's eyes on him, he gathered Almirez in his arms—whose body felt as light as a child's—and, with the help of two gringa women, loaded him into the back of his pickup.

Donny accelerated out of the parking lot, then checked his rearview mirror, where he could see the two women huddled over Almirez in the cargo bed, bouncing in the air whenever he hit a bump. Here he was, thought Donny, racing to the emergency room, when only moments before he was prepared to shoot the man—the irony not lost on him. The younger of the two women rapped hard on the rear window, her reddish hair whipping about her head. Donny slid open the glass. "Faster," she said, "they're coming!" Donny adjusted his rearview mirror to take in a line of jet-black vans in the distance—which he recognized from the morning before—pursuing them at great speed.

As he bounded over the desert, waves of dust enveloped them. How had he found himself in such a mess? At last, he reached the blacktop and gunned it, the engine straining.

"Hurry," the older woman cried, "he needs a doctor at once!" Donny could see her in the mirror take off her white cardigan and press it against Almirez's chest, staining it dark red.

One of the black vehicles was nearly upon them now, just a few hundred yards behind. Donny could hear the deep rumble of its engine. He looked down at the speedometer—105—amazed his truck could go that fast. Cresting a rise, Donny spotted the start of Durango's shantytown, a sprawling grid of dirt lanes and makeshift, multicolored homes. All of a sudden, a shot rang out and his rear window shattered, just inches from his head, as fine glittering particles, like mist, rained down upon him.

XVII.

Los Negros

The bullet passed so close to Catharine's face she could hear it go by. The moment it smashed through the truck's rear window, the driver stomped on the breaks and abruptly turned left down a narrow side road, heading into the heart of the slum. Behind them, the black van shot past, then a second later she heard the screech of its tires on asphalt. They barreled down the dirt lane, nearly running into a group of schoolchildren in uniforms. A dog yelped, scurrying out of the way. As she stared down at Almirez, now unconscious, she was astonished by how much she felt as tears welled up in her eyes, which the wind promptly swept away. They turned down an even narrower alley, barely clearing the walls on either side, going faster than seemed feasible. At the next intersection, the driver cut right, then immediately left, then slowed to a crawl. Catharine listened for the roar of the van's big engine, but heard nothing—only dogs, an occasional rooster. They idled past row after row of improvised structures, made of concrete and corrugated metal, plywood and plastic. The driver stopped and backed up until they were in front of the opening of a garage, then he inched his way into the dark, cramped space, empty except for a motorcycle against the wall. The driver switched off the ignition. No one moved for a moment—the engine ticking.

An old man appeared, barefoot and shirtless, with a scar running down the center of his chest, and began to shout at the driver. Catharine rose from the truck bed—"*¡Por favor, un doctor pronto!*"—and indicated Almirez at her feet.

The old man peered into the truck. "*¿Almirez?*" he asked, adopting a grievous air.

"*Sí,*" Catharine said, "*Almirez.*"

The man shook his head in disgust, then turned and hollered into the recesses of the house. Two women—a mother and daughter—emerged and wordlessly went about gathering sheets and towels, a bucket of water, and what appeared to be a first-aid kit. Meanwhile, the old man leapt onto his motorcycle and sped away.

The women worked hastily to locate and clean each wound. He had been hit in three places: his forearm, shoulder, and under his bottom left rib. The bullet seemed to have passed through in each case but one—beneath his rib. They drenched the wounds with alcohol then wrapped them tight with a white cloth.

Looking for the least sign of life and finding none, Catharine wondered out loud, "*¿Vivo?*"

"*Sí,*" the mother said. "*Pero apenas.*"

Before long, the old man returned on his motorcycle, accompanied by a white-bearded man wearing flip-flops, who Catharine assumed was the doctor. He injected Almirez in the hip with a long needle, then set up a drip into his arm, asking Brigitte to assist. Dutifully, she stood over Almirez, holding the sack of clear liquid, looking stoical even as tears rolled down her face.

Out of the silence, Catharine could make out the low rumble of the black van in the distance. The old man hurried to the opening of his garage and, as if reading her mind, lowered a huge tarp that covered the entrance and enveloped them in darkness.

"Better I speak in English, no?" the doctor said.

Catharine nodded.

"Much blood lost. And here . . ."—he pointed to the area just below the rib, shaking his head—" . . . he must go to the hospital."

"But how? They're waiting for him out there . . ." Catharine motioned toward the blazing street beyond the tarp.

Just then, a corner of the tarp pulled back and a small boy's face peered in. "¡*Oye! Vienen Los Negros*," he said, then the tarp closed again.

A few moments later, one of the vans arrived just outside the garage, the deep thunder of its motor idling past.

Everyone moved at once to the rear of the garage like a formation of birds and squatted behind the pickup—all except Brigitte, who remained standing in the bed of the truck, cradling the drip bag as if it were a newborn.

The vehicle came to a stop. Cab doors opened and shut. Catharine could hear men's voices barking back and forth. They knocked at the house next-door, then silence. One of the men struck the tarp from the outside so that it rippled loudly and Catharine jumped. As the tarp was slowly drawn back, a triangle of light appeared, and into this field of light stepped the silhouette of a man holding a gun.

XVIII.

Vigilantes

The tall man with the gun blinked a few times as his eyes adjusted to the darkness. Donny considered charging him, taking advantage of his disoriented state, but then hesitated and remained crouched behind the truck with the others. The man seemed surprised to find a red-haired girl standing in the back of a pickup holding a drip bag. They stared at one another, expressionless. In the muted light, Donny could make out his thin mustache and tailored black suit. The man continued to blink as if unsure of what he was seeing.

The tall Mexican then stepped forward and raised his gun toward the girl. "*¿Ese es el pedazo de mierda?*" he said.

Glaring down from the truck bed, she too stepped forward, full of defiance now, and positioned herself between Almirez and the gunman, holding the drip bag in one hand, the tubing in the other.

"*¡Fuera de aquí, carajo!*" the man commanded. But the girl would not move—squaring her stance instead. Donny felt a sudden rush of emotion, for how poised and brave she was, which in turn sparked a desire to protect her.

"*Verdammte Scheiße!*" she cried. "Why? *¿Por qué?* What do you want?"

"*¡Te dije, mueve tu puto culo!*"

Donny reached for his gun in the waistband of his jeans, as fear surged through him, and prepared for a charge.

"*¡Oye!*" came another voice from outside the garage—his accomplice. "*¿Qué pasa allí? ¡Hay gente aquí!*"

"*¿Gente?*" said the gunman, directing his voice to the street. "*Sí . . .*"

At once, the tarp was drawn back as light flooded the garage, momentarily blinding Donny. Gradually shapes began to form at the opening of the garage as his eyes readjusted: Men, perhaps thirty of them, stood with clubs, crowbars, shotguns, pistols, pipes . . . The other gunman already lay on the ground, motionless, one side of his head caved-in and bloody. Seeing this, the tall Mexican sank to his knees, making sure to adjust the pantlegs of his suit, and with some dignity placed his gun down before the neighbor-hood's band of vigilantes. With a matter-of-factness Donny found breathtaking, a wiry man in overalls stepped forward, picked up the gunman's pistol and shot him twice in the head. Donny felt a wave of nausea pass through him while taking in a string of short, frantic breaths. A pair of vigilantes then dragged the bodies away, stuffed them into the back of the black van and drove off, leaving nothing behind but two oval-shaped stains on the ground of drying blood.

Standing outside the garage now, Donny watched in astonishment as more and more gathered in the street—not just men, but women and children, old people as well, many with weapons. He saw a small boy who could barely stand upright wielding a plumber's wrench.

Just then, a second black van appeared, a moment later a third, their motors rumbling, the smell of diesel in the air. En masse, the mob then turned and advanced toward them, weapons raised, a half-dozen shotguns cocked in unison. The vehicles revved their engines, blared their horns. And yet the crowd continued to close in. A tinted passenger window slid down a few inches, from which emerged the barrel of a gun, and almost instantly a shot rang out from the street, pulverizing the glass. Tires spinning, the vehicles abruptly went into reverse, nearly running into each other, then turned a corner and vanished from sight.

Donny couldn't get over how the community had risen up so decisively against the cartel (or whoever they were) in defense of Almirez, who they clearly saw as some exalted folk hero. They turned amongst themselves, grinning and cheering and patting each other on the back. And Donny found himself smiling as well. For once, there was justice in the world: the bad guys had been defeated.

Their celebration went on for some time. And then, as if a cloud had passed over them, they started back for the garage and began to solemnly line up to pay their respects to Almirez.

Was he still alive? Donny wondered. He seemed to be, at least by the way the red-haired girl continued to stand over him. And what did they want from him now, now that he was on the verge of death? Someone had lowered the tailgate so that his bare feet lay exposed. One by one, they came up to him and touched and kissed his feet, dipped their fingers and pieces of clothing into the blood congealed in the bed of the truck. It was like they were taking communion, thought Donny—more than a little horrified—as they bowed and blessed themselves and brought their blood-stained fingers to their lips. They wept and whispered prayers, and when they walked away, many staggered or blinked their eyes, as if returning from some faraway place.

XIX.

The Serape

Gripping the sidewalls of the pickup, Catharine stared down at Almirez. He lay so perfectly still she was no longer certain he was still breathing. She and Brigitte kept looking at one another without saying a word, exchanging little glances that seemed to convey the unavoidable truth that Almirez was not long for this world. The bearded doctor, having climbed up into the cargo bed, now hovered over him, moving the diaphragm of his stethoscope from one region of his chest to another, pausing each time to listen. Word had apparently spread, and the tide of worshippers seemed endless. No one, thought Catharine, wanted to miss the moment of Almirez's passing, in the likelihood that it might one day become as holy as Christ's crucifixion.

The driver of the pickup came up beside her, an American with thinning black hair and melancholy eyes. "He's not going to make it, is he?"

Catharine shook her head, feeling a lump in her throat.

"What about the hospital?"

"It's too late for that . . ."

The doctor removed the stethoscope from his ears, reflecting a moment, then looked up at Brigitte. Catharine could not see the doctor's expression, though Brigitte's was one of utter desolation, as tears streamed down her cheeks. The doctor stood and gently took the drip bag from Brigitte's hands, and then together, holding onto one another, they climbed down from the truck. A great wail went out amongst the crowd and, like waves, repeated itself over and over again. The wife of the man who owned the garage brought an old black and white-striped serape and draped it over Almirez's body and face. Catharine felt a great pit open up inside her—a dark void without hope or purpose or light. But while Brigitte's tears could not be more justified than now, Catharine found she was unable to weep, as if her loss were too great. She sank to the concrete floor, crumpled sideways, with her head resting against the rusted chassis of the truck.

If not the Messiah, what was he? None of her questions had been answered. Nothing had been resolved. How could she go back to her old life now? The very existence of a divine order was in question. She could not allow herself to accept that life was nothing but randomness. And why had she come? What did God have in store for her, if anything? It had to be more than just getting in the way at the Hospice Center, grieving in the quiet hours for the child she gave away. Not since she was a small girl had she felt her faith come so alive . . . and now what?

From far off, she could hear the doctor's deep baritone calling out to the crowd: *"Es hora de irse. Por favor, vayanse ahora. Vayanse a sus casas."* He and the owner of the garage began to usher people out onto the street. As the crowd gradually dispersed, Catharine closed her eyes, in the hopes of shutting out the world.

AFTER AN INDETERMINATE TIME, she noticed that the garage was silent. She got up and looked around. No one was there but Almirez's prone figure in the back of the truck, the street cast in late-afternoon shadow. How long had she lain there?

From some distant, interior room, she could make out voices, strains of music. She proceeded down a long hallway, the music and voices growing louder, until she came upon a small room crowded with people, lit by a single bulb dangling from the ceiling. Everyone bellowed a greeting and raised their shot glasses as she appeared in the doorway. What was this—a wake, a celebration? On the table stood a nearly empty bottle of tequila and a transistor radio playing maria-chi. She spotted Brigitte and the American leaning together in a corner, glasses raised, Brigitte for once looking happy. Having commandeered the bottle, the doctor sat before the table distributing drinks. Someone handed Catharine a glass. She threw back the tequila without hesitation, shivering as it burned going down, and everyone applauded. She felt numb. She heard his name being passed around, almost cheerily—*Almirez*. Had they really moved on so soon?

The mother and daughter brought out trays piled with steaming tamales—refried beans oozing from the ends—and set them down on the table. They stepped back, pleased by the reception, as the room clapped and cheered, and a flurry of hands reached in. The old man who owned the garage, now in a white dress shirt, came up from behind and, with a degree of pride, hugged his ample wife and daughter. A second bottle of tequila materialized, and the doctor poured another round. They toasted the garage owner and his family for their hospitality and the blessing of having Almirez die in their home. After her second shot, Catharine felt a little woozy and had to steady herself against the doorframe.

A moment later, she noticed the small boy standing next to her, the same one who had warned them of *Los Negros*. He seemed upset, eager to speak. There was a certain resolve about the child—*chutzpah*, as her husband used to say. Cath-arine touched the boy's shoulder. "*¿Qué pasa?*" she asked.

"*Se ha ido,*" he said, "*se fue*"—as faces gradually turned and the room went quiet—"*Almirez se ha ido.*"

Catharine was unsure of what she just heard: did he just say *gone*?

Everyone moved at once, funneling out of the room, down the hall, and into the garage, until they all stood together before the pickup. Not daring to fully acknowledge it, Catharine felt a flutter inside of something like hope. She looked around at the staring faces. No one moved or said a word. There were thirteen of them altogether, including herself and the boy—thirteen witnesses. Despite the faint light, it was clear: Almirez had vanished from the cargo bed, and nothing remained but the crumpled black and white-striped serape.

XX.

The Sense of Things Having Come to an End

Donny had lost track of how many shots of tequila he'd had—four, maybe five? As he stood there in the garage with the others, he felt drunk and confused, trying to wrap his mind around the missing corpse. Perhaps one of Almirez's overzealous followers had taken the body, or the cartel had returned to carry him away—but to what end?

Rain began to fall, lightly at first then harder, and the wind picked up. A pair of chickens scampered across the front of the garage, stray feathers swirling in the air. The dirt road turned into a brownish-orange soup and rivulets ran down a slight hill and collected in a growing puddle at the intersection. The air cooled considerably; it was the first time Donny had felt cool in days. He was surprised to find he felt genuine grief at Almirez's death, and a degree of remorse. After all, he had hated the man—nearly killed him—blamed him for everything. He could see how that was unreasonable now, as if having woken from a long fever. He had no illusions that Almirez was some kind of saint, but he had seen how people were moved, how he inspired them. And when he closed his eyes now and tried to summon it, reaching deep inside, that long-standing hate had disappeared.

It was getting dark, and a chorus of generators kicked on, humming up and down the street, as lights streamed from the windows. The wife of the garage owner reached into the back of the truck and removed the serape, then with great care and reverence folded it into a neat square. There was the sense of things having come to an end. Everyone turned to one another as if looking for someone to take the lead, for what would come next. The doctor stared at the rear of Donny's truck, eyes unfocused, pulling meditatively on his white beard.

Donny thought of his ex-wife and children then, of getting back to them, and wondered how he might redeem himself after so many months of rage. He understood that the anger he felt for Maria, like the anger for Almirez, was an independent thing, like swallowing a red-hot coal, scorching everything inside.

He turned to the German girl, her arms crossed tightly over her chest, as if holding herself together. He couldn't help but feel drawn by the girl's boldness and curves and gently lopsided grin.

"I'm heading back to town now," he said.

She nodded and went to retrieve the American woman. Donny said *gracias* to the family and waved to the others, then climbed into his truck and started the engine. Then he waited as the older woman and German girl climbed into the cab as well—both looking glassy-eyed and stunned.

The doctor approached Donny's window with the boy by his side. "Better you take the boy with you," he said. "*¿Okey?* He'll guide you out of here and back to town . . . Name's Carlos: *un buen chico*, speaks a little English—an orphan like Almirez. You can give a few pesos if you like."

Donny agreed and the boy clambered into the cargo bed.

He backed out of the garage into the drizzly night, the streets abandoned. They drove a couple of blocks until the boy tapped on what remained of the rear window. "*Aquí . . .*" he said, pointing down an alley. "Go here."

Just as Donny was about to make the turn, he saw in his rearview mirror two black vans pull up and stop in front of the garage. Instantly, his heart hammered in his throat, and he stepped on the gas, fishtailing around the corner.

Moments later, he heard gunfire—round after round— echoing in the distance.

"What was that?" the American woman asked.

Donny shrugged, deciding it was better to say nothing, and drove on, his hands trembling on the steering wheel.

DESPITE THE WIPERS' frantic efforts, the rain peppering the windshield made everything a blur. The headlights swept over one ramshackle shack after another. The American woman asked Donny to stop, so that the boy could get in out of the rain. Donny did so and the drenched child squeezed into the cab between the two women. They continued on, winding their way through the maze of narrow muddy lanes. Finally, they reached the blacktop that cut through the desert toward town. The rain let up and Donny opened his window wide, savoring the cool night air. He felt suddenly optimistic, as if a fresh start had availed itself and he could put everything behind him now.

After a while, Donny's headlights lit up a small, disheveled figure in the distance, shuffling along in the middle of the road. Now what? thought Donny. As they drew near, Donny slowed down. It looked like an elderly man, his clothes sopping wet, his hair plastered to his head, and Donny could see, by the way the fellow drifted from side to side, that he must be a drunk.

Donny pulled up behind him and honked his horn. The man paused, interrupting his laborious progress. In the headlights, with his clothes clinging to him, he looked like a sculpture made of stone. His arms hung by his side and his feet were bare, the hems of his trousers dragging on the ground.

Donny yelled out of his window, "*Señor*—you need a ride?" Then he turned to the boy: "Carlos, how do you say *ride . . .?*" But when he saw the boy's face, he knew he wasn't listening— his eyes transfixed, staring straight ahead. Donny turned his attention back to the man and saw that he was facing them now, his shirt torn and spattered with what looked like dried blood, his torso crisscrossed with strips of darkly stained cloth. Then Donny gasped involuntarily, as the man who was once Almirez held them in a Lazarus-like stare.

XXI.

Bordo Poniente

From the truck bed, Catharine watched the desert speed past, a vast scrappy plane of ocotillos and creosote bushes. Wind whipped her hair and a bluish, pre-dawn light washed over the landscape. She huddled shivering in her sweater, stiff with Almirez's blood, as his body lay still at her feet.

It had been a long and remarkable night, well outside the reach of any reasonable reality: Had Almirez actually *risen* or had the doctor simply made a mistake? Had the drip bag revived him, or had he healed himself? And how had he covered such a distance—bleeding, with barely a pulse?

As she wrapped her arms around herself and stared down at the rusted metal floor of the truck bed, she tried to piece together the events of the previous night.

After the initial shock, they had hurried Almirez to a small clinic west of town, where they found a lone doctor asleep on a bench. Skinny and goateed, in a lab coat and jeans, he looked all of twenty-three. Catharine and Brigitte shook him awake and dragged him out to the truck.

Almirez sat slumped against the sidewall of the cargo bed, legs outstretched, staring at nothing. He looked utterly bewildered, as if reluctant to still be alive.

While the doctor took Almirez's vitals, he continued to shake his head. "*Debería estar muerto.*"

"What?" Catharine asked.

"He should be dead."

Catharine recognized that same glazed look on her husband's face near the end—of resignation and surrender.

At once, Almirez grabbed the doctor by the wrist and pulled him close, whispering in his ear. Catharine could not make out what he said, but the doctor nodded solemnly, then turned to her and shrugged. "He says no medicine . . . no treatment."

Almirez then looked imploringly from face to face—from the doctor to Catharine to Carlos to Brigitte—and finally rested his eyes on Donny. As if in a trance, he began to repeat the same phrase over and over again, "*Llévame a Bordo Poniente . . . llévame a Bordo Poniente . . .*"

Catharine knew enough to recognize what he was saying: Almirez wanted to return to the place where he was born—Bordo Poniente—the massive dumping ground outside Mexico City. She remembered reading about it, the largest landfill on the planet, visible even from space. Was he trying to fulfill some destiny, a prophesy perhaps—finishing where he began?

As everyone stared at Donny, he looked embarrassed, his long basset hound face furrowed and drawn. "What's he saying now?"

Catharine was relieved to see Brigitte step forward and take him aside. They stood together beneath a eucalyptus tree, heads tilted toward one another, the lights of the clinic casting them in silhouette.

A moment later Donny stepped back. "Really—are you serious? I'm not driving all the way . . . Hell, he'll be dead before . . ."

Brigitte continued to speak calmly, stroking his upper back as if he were a skittish horse. Catharine could see him soften under her touch, see something burgeoning between them. Finally, Brigitte embraced him and kissed him lightly on the cheek, as if in thanks, so that Donny came away amenable and flushed.

In this way, it was decided: Donny would drive them all to Bordo Poniente and take Almirez home.

DAWN WAS NEARLY UPON them now as the truck crossed the desert, slicing through the morning mist. Catharine continued to go over the evening in her mind, trying to preserve each moment like some modern-day apostle.

Throughout the night, as Almirez lay unconscious in the cargo bed, she had knelt beside him in a state of panic, expecting the worst, feeling for a pulse, some indication of his breath. She could see the others through the shattered rear window of the cab, a tableau of a happy family—Donny driving, Brigitte in the passenger seat, and Carlos in between. She was pleased to see Brigitte so content now, her tears all gone—almost flirtatious. Now and then she heard their voices and laughter above the tires and the wind.

At some point she must have fallen asleep, because when she looked at Almirez again he was sitting upright, head tilted back, staring up at the night sky. He looked perfectly calm and awake.

This man who seemed to have defied nature, the laws of mortality, who appeared to know the inner workings of her mind (of Zack's existence no less), who by his own assertion subsumed the universe—how was she to address him?

"*¿Señor . . . está bien?*"

An absurd question, she realized—after all, wasn't he supposed to be dead?

Almirez leveled his eyes upon her, then looked away. There was no feeling of transcendence, no unstruck sound, no profound vision of unity.

He began to deliver a speech, or perhaps a sermon, his first words jumbled and tongue-tied. Then they came out fast, as if by rote, without intonation, his eyes staring off into darkness. There was a vacancy about him—like Lazarus, she imagined, after Jesus brought him back to life: the lights were on, but no one was home.

His monologue went on for some time. Now and then he would pause to rub abstractedly at his wounds. Catharine listened rapt, anxious not to miss anything, suspecting that the mysteries of the universe, known only to the enlightened, were being revealed—and yet all lost to her. An entire cosmology she failed to hear or understand. Above the sound of the engine, she could only pick up a smattering of words ... *Blood ... Light ... Destroy ... Repent ... Suffocate ... Silence ... Surrender ...* and then a phrase: "*Todo está perdonado*" *(all is forgiven)*. If he had in fact returned from the dead, was this the reason why—to give a speech? And who was it for anyway? Was it intended for her? And why would *she* be the witness (someone with high school-level Spanish)? But perhaps that was the point: it wasn't meant to be fully understood. For all Catharine knew, they could have been the ramblings of a lunatic.

The pick-up steadily climbed as Almirez spoke, zigzagging its way up the mountainside, the air growing cooler by the minute. Pine trees lined the lower slopes, towering presences that cut off starlight; and then, as if a curtain had parted, the luminous sky reappeared. They continued to climb until somewhere high up in the Sierra Madre, as the truck wound its way along sheer cliffs and stars wielded overhead like fireworks, his voice faltered, and he fell silent.

A moment later, Almirez curled up into a fetal position and moaned, shuddering in pain. As Catharine drew near, he reached out and took hold of her skirt and cried *"¡Madre!"* fixing his eyes upon her. It was but one word, and yet she felt a profound welling up of emotion. She understood their symbiotic connection almost at once: while he was an orphan who had never known his mother, she was a mother who had never known her child. And now he needed her . . . not as some saintly figure, but a vulnerable human being. She stroked his forehead, pushing his bangs back from his eyes, and whispered, *"Todo va a estar bien."* But then she heard the word *"Madre"* echo once again in her mind and wondered if he had meant something more . . . Had Almirez, in a delirium, mistaken Catharine for his mother, or was he somehow appointing her as such and, thereby, making her . . . what exactly? *"La" Madre*—the essence of Marianismo, the Virgin of Guadalupe, the Aztec Coatlicue? A crazy thought (even symbolically). She shuddered and closed her eyes, feeling the truck begin its descent as it followed one switchback after another. Darkness swept over and around her like a river. She held onto the sidewall, still cradling Almirez's head, then noticed how utterly still he was. When she felt for his pulse, she realized he was gone.

SITTING NOW IN THE BACK of the pickup, bathed in pastel light, Catharine considered Almirez's motionless figure and wept. But was he truly gone? And now that he had presumably performed the feat, was there really any point in doing it again? She still felt unsure whether Almirez was the Messiah or not—perhaps she would never know—but perhaps it no longer mattered. She knew his legacy would be explained away, turned into a joke—the curious tale of a mad conman and drifter who deceived a nation. As the desert sped past, Catharine shivered in the wind. Now and then a lone cactus appeared on the horizon, its arms extended like some Hindu deity. Gutted and forlorn, she clung to her bloodstained sweater, until somewhere south of León she got up and banged on the roof, then yelled into the cab through the shattered window.

"He's gone."

"What?" cried Donny.

"Almirez is dead."

Donny nodded, Brigitte as well. Carlos turned and stared at her with his big molasses eyes, studying her to see what to feel. No one seemed terribly concerned or impressed. The pickup remained on course. What were they doing traipsing across Mexico with a corpse? Suddenly it all seemed pointless. And yet they continued toward Bordo Poniente—to fulfill the promise to a dead man.

FROM FAR OFF, Catharine spotted the landfill, a great sprawling mountain range of trash, as smoke billowed around it and dawn rose blazing behind it. As they drew near, it continued to grow to monstrous proportions—some peaks, obscured by clouds, invisible from below. They followed a dirt road that sloped downward, passing on either side a bustling shantytown, until they came to a large muddy cul-de-sac. The stench of rot and decay hit her like an olfactory wall. Old sofas and tires, car chassis and refrigerators, an undulating sea of plastic, the brazen scuttling of rats, pools of bubbling sludge, the festering remains of a thousand cabbage heads and fly-crazed fruit rinds, the carcass of an unidentifiable animal—the whole foul display extended for as far as she could see. And now what? thought Catharine, as there was still the matter of the body to consider. Perhaps his people would gather, drawn by some invisible force, and mark the loss of their fallen son. But, in the end, no one came, except an old man with a cane, who hobbled over, peered into the back of the truck, and walked away.

They all climbed out of the pickup and stretched and stood side-by-side at the edge of the dump in silence. Brigitte reached out and took Donny's hand, Catharine was pleased to see, while Carlos found a soccer ball, shredded but still intact, and began juggling it with his knees and feet.

At last, Catharine saw her purpose, how to devote herself, where she was needed—suddenly it was clear . . . She would relocate herself and Zack, build a sanctuary of sorts (perhaps in this very village). And Carlos would need a home, of course, a good school. . . .

As the sun continued to climb, Catharine looked out over the smoldering expanse, taking it all in, this place where Almirez was improbably born. There was so much to do, but for now she could only marvel at the great swirl of life, as dogs and scavenger birds and giant excavation machines crisscrossed the ridge. And a small child waded knee-deep into the trash as if entering the sea.

Acknowledgments

Gratefully acknowledged are the following publications, where certain stories first appeared:

"The Prince of Denmark" in *Prime Number Magazine, The Doire Press International Chapbook Competition Anthology* (in a different version), and *Storyglossia* (in a different version as the "The Leap")

"In the German Garden" in *upstreet* and *Everywhere Stories: Short Fiction from a Small Planet: Vol. 1*

"Sumo" in *Mid-American Review*

"Sane" in *Lumina*

"French Windows" in *upstreet* and *Upstairs at Duroc*

"Shooting with Helmut" in *CutBank*

"Lan and Jin" in *Hunger Mountain Review*

"Mejdoub" in *Gulf Stream*

"Mykonos (circa 1988)" in *Prime Number Magazine* and *Prime Number Magazine, Editor's Selections: Vol. 3*.

* * *

Many thanks to my infinitely patient and wise first readers: Cathy Albano, Patricia Kauffmann, Malcolm Campbell, and Joachim Lüning. Heartfelt gratitude to those rare and brilliant teachers who inspired me: Eva Szekeres, Kermit Moyer, Gurumayi, Thomas Absher, Sue Silverman, Frank Bidart, James Salter, Frank Conroy, and Leonard Michaels. Profound thanks as well to Jack, Patricia, and Bruce Kauffmann, who kindled in me a love of literature. Much gratitude to Dr. Ross Tangedal and Cornerstone Press for their faith in my writing, to Amber Marley Padilla and Diane Lefer for their Spanish proofreading, and to Thomas Feiner for his striking, visionary cover art. And my sincere appreciation to those organizations that provided support during the writing of this book: Randolph College, WriterHouse, and Konstepidemin (The Epidemic of Art).

Note: some liberties were taken concerning where saguaros grow.

JAY KAUFFMANN is a former international model, travel writer, and award-winning poet. He holds an MFA from Vermont College of Fine Arts and is currently English Chair at the Miller School of Albemarle. Runner-up for the Leapfrog Global Fiction Prize and nominee for a Pushcart Prize and Best New American Voices, he has published in *CutBank*, *Prime Number*, *The Writer's Chronicle*, *upstreet*, *Mid-American Review*, and other journals and anthologies.

www.ingramcontent.com/pod-product-compliance
Lightning Source LLC
Chambersburg PA
CBHW031052310726
48969CB00007B/2244